JOHN M. ELLIS, MD
JEAN PAMPLIN

AVERY PUBLISHING GROUP
Garden City Park • New York

The therapeutic procedures in this book are based on the training, personal experiences, and research of the authors. Because each person and situation are unique, the author and publisher urge the reader to check with a qualified health professional before using any procedure when there is any question regarding appropriateness.

The publisher does not advocate the use of any particular diet or health program, but believes the information presented in this book should be available to the public.

Because there is always some risk involved, the authors and publisher are not responsible for any adverse effects or consequences resulting from the use of any of the suggestions, preparations, or procedures described in this book. Please do not use the book if you are unwilling to assume the risk. Feel free to consult with a physician or other qualified health professional. It is a sign of wisdom, not cowardice, to seek a second or third opinion.

Cover designer: Eric Macaluso
In-house editor: Elaine Will Sparber
Typesetters: Helen Contoudis and Gary Rosenberg
Printer: Paragon Press, Honesdale, PA

Avery Publishing Group
120 Old Broadway
Garden City Park, NY 11040
1–800–548–5757

Illustrations on pages 7, 48, 52, 71, 72, and 103 drawn by Lucille Ellis.

Library of Congress Cataloging-in-Publishing Data

Ellis, John Marion, 1917–
    Vitamin B_6 therapy : nature's versatile healer / by John M. Ellis
and Jean Pamplin.
        p.   cm.
    Includes bibliographical references
    ISBN 0-89529-866-X
    1. Vitamin B_6—Therapeutic use.   2. Vitamin B_6—Physiological
effect.   I. Pamplin, Jean.   II. Title.
RM666.V57E45 1999
615'.328—dc21   98-381
                                                                                  C

Printed in the United States of America.

10 9 8 7 6 5 4 3 2 1

CONTENTS

This book is dedicated to the physicians, surgeons, and scientists who persevere in the delivery of proper nutrition to people of all ages in need.

PREFACE

Since its discovery in 1934, vitamin B_6 has become the most researched vitamin on earth. Once in the body, vitamin B_6 is transformed into pyridoxal phosphate, a coenzyme responsible for activating enzymes and enzyme systems. Virtually every bodily activity depends upon proper enzyme action. Without sufficient pyridoxal phosphate present in the body, enzymes cannot function. Even the biochemical action that controls protein metabolism depends upon vitamin B_6—an important note for today's high-protein consumer. The main purpose in writing and publishing this book is to inform readers in clear and concise language about disease conditions that can be prevented by taking a daily vitamin-B_6 supplement. Years of extensive clinical analysis and laboratory experimentation have gone into making this book the most comprehensive available on vitamin B_6, also known as pyridoxine.

Vitamin B_6 has gained widespread attention in the treatment of disease conditions including coronary heart disease, diabetes, carpal tunnel syndrome, complications of pregnancy, and soft-tissue rheumatism. The scientific literature includes scores of cases and examples in which patients showed marked improvement during and after B$_6$ therapy. Physicians and scientists have demonstrated that the human body requires the combined action of folic acid, vitamin B$_6$, and vitamin B$_{12}$ for the proper control of homocysteine, which is now accepted as a risk factor for arteriosclerosis and coronary heart disease, the leading cause of death in the United States today. This complex relationship to the deadly heart attack is discussed in detail in Chapter 6, "Diabetes," and Chapter 7, "Coronary Heart Disease." Other chapters dissect the relationship of vitamin B$_6$ to carpal tunnel syndrome, gynecologic and obstetric disorders, arthritis and rheumatism, and brain function.

In 1961, I began clinical studies of human vitamin-B$_6$ deficiency. Over a period of seventeen years, I sent tubes of blood samples packed in ice from my clinic in Mt. Pleasant, Texas, to Professor Karl Folkers, Ph.D., director of the Institute for Biomedical Research at the University of Texas at Austin. Together, Dr. Folkers and I proved that sixteen signs and symptoms of vitamin-B$_6$ deficiency correlate with low specific activity of an enzyme in human blood. Describing these findings constitutes a driving force behind the publication of this book. Vitamin-B$_6$ deficiency is rampant in the United States.

INTRODUCTION

In the seventeenth century, an English physician, William Harvey, discovered how blood circulates in the heart, arteries, and veins. His book *An Anatomical Treatise on the Motion of the Blood in Animals*, published in 1628, became a cornerstone of medicine. The scientific community both embraced and expanded his theory of circulation and the circulatory system, and today the whole concept is common knowledge. Perhaps someone in the future will discover how to manufacture great men from ordinary children, much like bees transform a common larva into a queen. Bees use royal jelly, a special food they prepare. If such a food existed for humans, I would warrant that it included ample amounts of vitamin B_6. Although no one completely understands the complexities of the nutrients flowing through the body's rivers of life, there is probably no single nutrient more involved in the myriad processes of health than this often-overlooked member of the B-complex family.

When you think of vitamin B_6 and the enzymatic reactions in which it is involved, you have to think of all the systems in the body. More than a thousand scientific articles concerning vitamin B_6 and its relationship to the very complex chemistries of the human body have been published in prestigious English-language journals alone. The list of metabolic functions that cannot take place properly without the assistance of sufficient vitamin B_6 includes the synthesis (formation) of protein to repair worn-out tissue, the production of antibodies to fight infection, and the proper metabolism (breaking down) of fat to prevent the accumulation of cholesterol. Over twenty years ago, the man who discovered and named vitamin B_6, Dr. Paul György, announced that "to prevent many common and serious illnesses of advanced age, people ought to be taking 10 times as much B_6 as most of us do!"[1]

We think of ourselves as immune to the barbaric nutritional diseases of the past such as scurvy, beriberi, and pellagra, but it is in our sterile, beautiful store aisles that we must be the most alert, for the very heat and cold that prolong the shelf lives of our food products strip away their nutrients. The National Research Council has set the Recommended Dietary Allowance (RDA) of vitamin B_6 for normal people at 2 milligrams, suggesting that this amount consumed daily is sufficient to maintain health.[2] Yet most people don't get even that much. At Tuskegee Institute in Alabama over a period of three consecutive years, women with toxemia of pregnancy, also called pregnancy-induced hypertension (PIH), showed a vitamin-B_6 intake of only 43 to 48 percent of the RDA.[3]

It has been my experience in thirty-plus years of clinical research that vitamin B_6, also known as pyridoxine, is effective therapy for carpal tunnel syndrome. Vitamin B_6 can reduce the effects of such debilitating diseases as diabetes and the deadly heart attack. The painful swelling of arthritis and pregnancy-related edema disappear under a regimen of vitamin-B_6 therapy. Even brain function is affected by the important role that vitamin B_6 plays in maintaining or reestablishing the healthy biochemical actions of that marvelous machine, the human body.

I have found that in a great majority of cases, carpal tunnel syndrome is relieved when 200 milligrams of vitamin B_6 is taken daily for ninety days. This treatment works equally well for men and women. The treatment may be instituted at any stage during the development of the syndrome, but it is most effective when the numbness and tingling first develop in the hands and fingers. The quicker the B_6 treatment is begun, the better are the results.

I have proven that up to 300 milligrams of vitamin B_6 taken daily is a safe and necessary health guard for pregnant women and diabetic adults.[4] Pregnant women need supplemental B_6 to offset the increase in steroid hormones during pregnancy, to relieve edema, and to ensure the health and proper development of the fetus. In a study of 225 pregnant women over a nine-year period, it was found that B_6 also brought relief to the 11 percent of subjects who suffered from carpal tunnel syndrome.[5] Diabetic patients need vitamin B_6 to help prevent the excessive union of excess blood sugar with the protein residues from amino acids such as tryptophan and methionine.[6–8] In the presence of high blood sugar, there is a leakage of fatty streaks and fluid into the retina at the back of the eye, which leads to diabetic blindness. Vitamin B_6 is a factor in the prevention of this blindness.[9,10]

Steroid hormones produced by the ovaries and adrenal glands are extremely important in the biochemistries of women, both just before menstruation and at menopause. Estrogen, including that found in birth control pills, affects women on a monthly basis. Premenstrual edema (swelling in the hands and feet) is relieved by a daily dose of 200 milligrams of B_6 taken indefinitely. Daily vitamin-B_6 treatment can also prevent a type of premenstrual rheumatism found in some women's shoulders, arms, and hands.[11] Women have a normal and delicate balance of hormones, hormones that to some extent enter into all the different tissues of the body, the uterine and breast tissues in particular. At menopause, these hormones decrease in amount and menstruation ceases. This menopausal deficiency also very often shows up as swelling and stiffness in the fingers and hands. Vitamin B_6 given at a dosage of 200 milligrams daily for an indefinite period of time will prevent as well as cure this menopausal arthritis.

This relationship of vitamin B$_6$ to the steroid hormones, including cortisone, has led to the further discovery that advanced or prolonged vitamin-B$_6$ deficiency in both men and women contributes to the stiffness, loss of flexibility, and pain of rheumatism and degenerative arthritis that have always been associated with the aging process. Vitamin B$_6$ preserves the normal function of the synovium, cartilage, nerves, and tendons around the joints of the knees, shoulders, elbows, and hands.

Coronary heart disease is the leading cause of death in the United States. The deadly heart attack, also known as myocardial infarction, occurs when the arteries supplying blood to the heart undergo change, harden, and calcify. Atherosclerosis (hardening of the arteries via the buildup of fatty deposits) and arteriosclerosis (hardening of the arteries via the buildup of calcium deposits) begin in childhood and lead eventually to heart attack, especially in younger men. Vitamin B$_6$ preserves the elastic fibrils (very small fibers) in the large arteries, including the aorta.[12,13]

Back in 1961, the suspected connection between cholesterol and heart disease inadvertently contributed to my clinical research proving that vitamin-B$_6$ therapy is instrumental in keeping the arteries healthy. Like every doctor, I read the reports and decided to urge my patients to follow the recommendations for lowering cholesterol. I rationalized that food has both a direct and indirect bearing upon one's physical condition, and it certainly seemed sensible to encourage my patients to limit their intake of saturated fats. The average American diet at that time consisted of almost 50-percent fats. This, coupled with the high rate of heart attacks, gave me no reason to doubt the cholesterol theory.

I studied several different medical diets available at the time and finally opted for a low-fat diet developed by Dr. Lester M. Morrison at the College of Medical Evangelists in

Los Angeles. Patients who had been consuming a high-fat diet and experiencing muscle spasms and tingling in their limbs found themselves cured after going on the Morrison diet. Most significant to me, however, was the fact that the pain and tingling in the limbs resolved, and all the participants stated that they had improved flexibility in their hands and fingers. These statements piqued my curiosity. I prescribed the Morrison diet as a hopeful aid against heart attacks, yet other symptoms responded. I realized that my patients had not eaten balanced diets prior to going on the Morrison diet, so obviously the results were due to more than the elimination of fats.

My doubts about the cholesterol theory increased after a mundane occurrence—the kitchen sink in my house became stopped up. The plumber told my wife to stop putting greasy water down the drain or we would continue having the problem. However, after he extracted three bucketfuls of tree roots from the sewer pipe, I pointed out that the roots were the culprit—the grease only compounded the problem by clinging to the roots in the pipe. After some reflection, I realized that most medical professionals were jumping to a premature conclusion just like the plumber. The plumber blamed the grease when, in reality, the initial cause was the tree roots in the pipe. Similarly, medical professionals blamed cholesterol for heart disease when it was really diseased arteries that were at fault. Only after an artery became diseased would an elevated serum-cholesterol level become a consideration, which led me to the all-important question: What was really causing the disease in the arteries?[14]

Subsequent research, as documented in this book, led me to vitamin B_6 and the conclusion that a human body lacking in vitamin B_6 is not in proper working order. Rather, that body is in ill health, and the severity of the disorder depends on the degree of the B_6 deficiency. In a land where more protein is eaten than in virtually any other nation on earth, what stands out as most significant is that vitamin B_6 is the "protein vitamin"—that is, it is the nutrient without which protein cannot be properly utilized.[15]

Biochemist R.R. Brown of the University of Wisconsin has suggested, "Although this vitamin is widely distributed in a variety of foods, its content in foods eaten by a weight conscious population may be rather marginal." Brown has also said that even adequate intake of vitamin B_6 may not be sufficient. There are a number of factors that lead to tissue deficiency including impaired delivery of the vitamin and excessive loss of the vitamin through excretion or inactivation by chemicals or drugs.[16] Enzymatic defects may also be involved.[17]

Vitamin B_6 is not the only nutrient necessary for the prevention or treatment of disease. Although there is clearly a B_6-deficiency disease, the body subsists on a delicate balance of a great number of vitamins and minerals, many of which act and interact with B_6. If a patient is B_6 deficient, he or she may very likely be deficient in other vitamins and minerals as well. This has been shown to be especially true of magnesium. Establishing the optimum amount of nature's nutrients for human health is a fascinating challenge.

If you experience pain, numbness, or tingling in your shoulders, arms, or hands, you are probably deficient in vitamin B_6. If you have stiffness and/or loss of flexion (bending) in the joints of your shoulders, arms, or hands, you are a candidate for B_6 therapy. If you have carpal tunnel syndrome, diabetes mellitus type I (insulin-dependent or juvenile diabetes) or type II (non-insulin-dependent diabetes), diabetic blindness, coronary heart disease, pregnancy-related edema, premenstrual edema, atherosclerosis, arteriosclerosis, menopausal arthritis, or painful degenerative arthritis in the knees, shoulders, arms, or hands, you need immediate B_6 treatment. All of these conditions respond positively when treated with varying daily doses of vitamin B_6.

The proof is substantial. In the early stages of my research, I asked my wife, Lucy, a commercial artist, to use her skills to draw what we termed the Quick Early Warning (QEW) sign of vitamin-B_6 deficiency. She drew hand after hand with the fingers bent at the middle joints, but unable to touch the top of the palm of the hand. (See Figure 1.) She recorded those same hands after B_6 treatment, bent to perfection, fingertips touching the top of the palm, no straining, just a natural, healthy reflex. My descriptions of these cases of finger- and joint-flexibility loss were the first ever to associate crippling of the hands with vitamin-B_6 deficiency, the degree of crippling and stiffness being related to the severity and duration of the vitamin-B_6 deficiency.

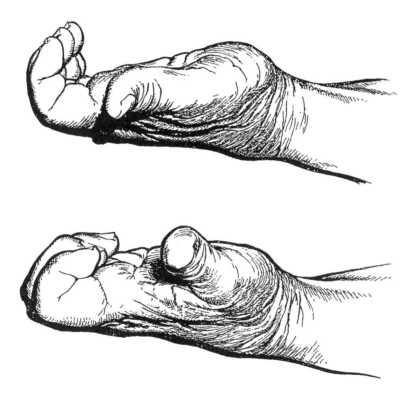

Figure 1. A dairyman's hand. Top illustration: Before vitamin-B_6 treatment, with his wrist and hand extended, this dairyman could not flex his fingers enough to touch the top of the palm of his hand. Bottom illustration: After taking 50 milligrams of vitamin B_6 daily for twenty-one days, he could.

In the human body, proteins are composed of twenty amino-acid building blocks. Recently, the amino acid methionine has received a great deal of attention because it produces homocysteine, a substance that has been directly linked to coronary heart disease. Methionine is one of nineteen amino-acid building blocks that are dependent upon vitamin B$_6$ to function properly. Vitamin B$_6$, vitamin B$_{12}$, and folic acid are necessary for the metabolic changes that reduce the toxic blood levels of homocysteine. This fact alone elevates the importance of vitamin B$_6$, but combined with the other information found in this book, and in a thousand other scientific articles, it makes vitamin B$_6$ the real breakthrough in modern medicine. The world continues to experience, but with even greater intensity, what vitamin-B$_6$-discoverer Paul György decades ago called "an almost explosive interest in the metabolic role of vitamin B$_6$ in man."[18]

Chapter 1

The Importance of Vitamin B$_6$

I have always believed that a doctor should do more than merely treat the obvious symptoms of disease. He or she should also guide patients in taking preventive measures, advising them on diet and personal habits that enhance rather than endanger health. And like every doctor and research scientist in the world, I have struggled for answers. There is one major difference between my conclusions and those reached by other researchers. Most other researchers base their findings purely on laboratory experiments, whereas I base my conclusions on my experiences with the patients in my clinic. And just as the blocked sewer pipe to my house stimulated my thinking, so have my patients guided me over the years into areas of concern that I could never have found in a laboratory situation. An example is the stiffness and tingling in my patients' hands. Did these symptoms have something to do with arteriosclerosis? Were they symptoms of some other factor involved in heart disease? Or, were they symptoms of another condition entirely?

As my files grew and my research material expanded from a few cases to dozens and then to hundreds, I found my interests directed toward the quantitative biochemistries of vitamin B$_6$. The more my patients responded to therapeutic doses of this vitamin, the more I became convinced of its importance.

In 1989, the U.S. Food and Drug Administration (FDA) set the U.S. Recommended Daily Allowances (USRDAs) of vitamin B$_6$ for normal people in good health. The nutrient values set included 0.3 milligram for infants six to eleven months of age, 1.0 milligram for children nine to thirteen years of age, 1.5 milligrams for females fourteen to eighteen years of age, 1.7 milligrams for males fourteen to eighteen years of age, 2.2 milligrams for pregnant females, and 2.0 milligrams for adult males.[1] The requirements for the elderly are the same as for adult males, yet the U.S. Department of Agriculture (USDA) Human Nutrition Research Center on Aging at Tufts University in Boston has revealed the need of the elderly to be 3.0 milligrams of vitamin B$_6$ daily.[2] How, then, can we tell if we are getting the correct amount of the nutrient?

The scientific truth is that millions of people need greater amounts of vitamin B$_6$ in their bodies than they can possibly get from the normal diet. Eaten in one day, one pound of fresh bananas, one pound of broiled lean beef, six slices of whole-wheat bread, and one cup of whole cow's milk provide a total of only 3.872 milligrams of B$_6$. To digest and metabolize the amino acid tryptophan in a piece of lean beefsteak, the body needs not only vitamin B$_6$, but also three different enzymes, all finely balanced with one another. If the vitamin B$_6$ is deficient, the body cannot properly metabolize the beefsteak. Today's popular high-protein diets therefore especially require the adequate intake of vitamin B$_6$.

Why is vitamin B$_6$ so wonderful as a preventive-healthcare therapy? Because of its function in the body. Once B$_6$ is taken into the body, it is transformed into pyridoxal phosphate. Pyridoxal phosphate is a conenzyme, a substance that functions to activate (set into motion) enzymes and enzyme systems. Enzymes trigger virtually every activity within our bodies. Without sufficient pyridoxal phosphate present to activate them, important enzymes cannot function properly. Altogether, 118 enzymes in the human body depend on vitamin B$_6$. Amino acids also need B$_6$ to function. There are 20 amino acids in the human body, and 19 of them require B$_6$.

Over and over, we find that disease-stressed bodies are highly in need of supplemental-B$_6$ therapy.[3] But even healthy people in the United States, young and old alike, suffer from vitamin deficiencies. A survey in the Boston area revealed that 65 percent of older adults living on their own took in less than two-thirds of the USRDAs for vitamins B$_6$, B$_{12}$, and D, as well as for folic acid, zinc, calcium, and chromium.[4] Researchers continue to prove that nutrients are not only necessary, but increased amounts used as therapy may actually prevent disease.

In a study I conducted along with Kilmer S. McCully, a pathologist at the Veterans Medical Center in Providence, Rhode Island, on the prevention of myocardial infarction by vitamin-B$_6$ therapy, the data I collected between the years of 1988 and 1992 show that among the elderly patients I treated, the average age at death of the patients who had taken vitamin B$_6$ was 84.5 years. Among my patients who did not take vitamin B$_6$ or who had taken vitamin B$_6$ for less than one year, the average age at death was 76.7 years. Among the patients of other physicians, none of whom had taken vitamin B$_6$, the average age at death was 74.0 years.[5]

Biochemists have demonstrated, without question, a relationship between vitamin B$_6$ and hormones including the steroid hormones. Minute amounts of B$_6$ can regulate, block, and even remove trace amounts of steroid hormones in a normal person. During pregnancy, if the mother-to-be is B$_6$ deficient, the huge amounts of estrogen and progesterone that her body produces become altered because the vitamin is not present in sufficient quantity to block abnormal binding of deoxyribonucleic acid (DNA) for gene expression. In other words, an expectant mother must have adequate vitamin B$_6$ in order for her estrogen and progesterone to have normal activity in the cells of her body, in her uterus in particular. Over a nine-year period, my treatment of 225 pregnant women with supplemental B_6 improved their pregnancy-related edema and severe symptoms of carpal tunnel syndrome.

As already mentioned, to metabolize the amino acid tryptophan, the body needs three enzymes, all of which depend on vitamin B_6 to complete their chains of actions. Other investigators have reported finding xanthurenic acid, a product in the chain of tryptophan metabolism, present in excessive amounts in the urine of expectant mothers with toxemia of pregnancy. Diabetes worsens vitamin-B_6 deficiency during pregnancy.[6]

Lysine, an amino acid found in fish, has a particular affinity for vitamin B_6 because B_6 helps bring lysine to the collagen and elastin in connective tissue, cartilage in joints, synovium around tendons, and matrix between cells. During research using B_6-deficient chickens, it was proven that B_6 is a cofactor of lysyl oxidase, another enzyme, thus verifying that prolonged vitamin-B_6 deficiency in humans causes crippling in the joints, particularly the knees, and in the aorta, which becomes subject to aneurysms (balloon-like swellings in the artery walls).[7-9]

In the presence of high blood sugar, glucose fractions (chemical components) link more with protein fractions, and the little enzymes cannot prevent it. Vitamin-B_6 therapy to a significant degree prevents this nonenzymatic glycosylation from happening with the very important proteins in the human body. These proteins include hemoglobin, which carries oxygen in the red blood cells, and immunoglobulin G, which functions as an antibody that helps to cure or combat bacterial and infectious diseases.[10-12] For this reason, 300 milligrams of vitamin B_6 should be taken daily by diabetic adults, and 50 milligrams should be taken daily by diabetic children.

Over seventy-five years ago, vitamin B_6 was first isolated. Forty-five years ago, it was conclusively proven to be essential to the normal functioning of the human body, to brain function, and to life itself. Remarkable research conducted by individuals and institutions has attested to the importance of B$_6$ and continues to be documented. In 1995, findings suggested that consumption of vitamin B$_6$, a precursor of pyridoxal phosphate, a coenzyme in amino-acid metabolism, reduces the risk of myocardial infarction in susceptible individuals.[13]

The key event that related hyperhomocysteinemia (the presence of excessive amounts of homocysteine in the blood) to vitamin-B$_6$ deficiency and arteriosclerosis was the discovery of arteriosclerotic lesions in children with inherited enzymatic disorders of homocysteine metabolism.[14] The homocysteine theory of arteriosclerosis was developed to explain the experimental, pathophysiological, clinical, and epidemiological characteristics of atherosclerosis.[15,16] In this theory, the declining incidence of death from myocardial infarction in the United States since 1965 is related to the increased consumption of synthetic vitamin B$_6$.[17]

Pyridoxal phosphate is the coenzyme of cystathionine synthase, the enzyme that converts homocysteine, an atherogenic amino acid, to cystathionine, a nonatherogenic amino acid. The metabolites (products of metabolism) of cystathionine—including cysteine, cysteine sulfinic acid, taurine, and sulfate—are also nonatherogenic. Vitamin B$_6$ reduces the risk of thromboembolism (the condition in which an embolism forms in one part of the circulation, becomes detached, and lodges in another part of the circulation) in those patients with cystathionine-synthase deficiency and homocystinuria (excessive excretion of homocysteine in the urine) who respond to vitamin-B$_6$ therapy.[18] Vitamin-B$_6$ therapy and a low-animal-protein diet counteract hyperhomocysteinemia, improve the clinical symptoms of angina, increase exercise tolerance, improve electrocardiogram (ECG) abnormalities, and improve glucose tolerance in patients with coronary heart disease.[19]

Simply put, vitamin B_6 is an essential vitamin that is in short supply in food. Today's refined food products encourage B_6 deficiency. To prove my point, I submit a case history reaching back to an era just prior to the modern supermarket revolution—harder times, but healthier. Prior to the Civil War, a teenaged African slave lived with my family in eastern Texas. During the war, at age nineteen, my Grandfather Ellis joined the Texas Brigade and rode for four years with the Texas Cavalry in the Confederate Army. When my grandfather returned to Texas, the newly freed young African-American took my family's surname of Ellis and rode with my grandfather to raise cattle, mules, and hogs in the White Oak and Sulphur River bottoms. Sam Ellis and my grandfather became lifelong friends.

In 1886, Sam married a young woman named Mary Ann. It was Sam and Mary Ann's daughter Annie who gave birth, in a log cabin, to twenty-one infants including three sets of twins. This was phenomenal. Annie had no abortions or miscarriages. She had her first child when she was eighteen years of age. From 1886 to 1910—over a twenty-four year period—Annie was pregnant eighteen times. Not one time was a physician present at the birth. All the infants were delivered by Annie's aunt, Mary Ann's sister Roxanna, the same woman who had delivered my father when he was born on December 3, 1885.

Annie had married a stable, intelligent young man. In clear handwriting, her husband, Major Simmons, recorded the name and date of birth of each of his children in the flyleaf of a Bible. The majority of the Simmons children lived for more than eighty years, and three lived to be more than one hundred years of age. In 1983, four of the children were still in Titus County, Texas, and my wife and I remained friends with them.

One evening when John Simmons had dinner with my wife and me, we talked about old times. I asked John, "What foods did you eat when you were a child?"

He answered, "We ate wild animals, birds, meat, and vegetables from the garden, but most of our food was what the hogs ate."

"What was that?" I asked.

"Hog shorts," John said. "That was the only kind of bread that we ate, and the food that we ate the most of."

"Hog shorts" was the term used for the milled shavings from wheat. In 1912, Casimir Funk, a Polish-born biochemist doing research in London, established that consuming only polished rice (shucked rice hulls) caused beriberi in pigeons. Using 836 pounds of unpolished rice, he separated the antiberiberi factor, which subsequently came to be known as vitamin B$_1$ (thiamine). Thereafter, vitamin research led to further discoveries. But for our purposes here, before and during her pregnancies, Annie ate the best source of naturally occurring vitamin B on earth. Then she fed her children the same food. Today, 93 percent of the vitamin B$_6$ in white bread made from wheat in the United States is destroyed during baking.[20]

In short, enzymes are in the cells of all the different organs in the human body. These more than one hundred enzymes depend on vitamin B$_6$ to complete their prescribed biochemical actions in these cells. If vitamin B$_6$ is not there in sufficient quantity to do its job day after day, the resulting products of split protein molecules become unhealthy and lead to disease.

Chapter 2

HOW VITAMIN B$_6$ WORKS

Because of the magnificent actions of vitamin B$_6$ in the human body, it is important to know just exactly what the vitamin is and how it works. To begin, let us discuss food as we know it. All food is made up of fat, protein, and/or carbohydrate (sugars and starch). Milk, for example, has all three elements. Once taken into the stomach, food is separated into these components by digestion. The stomach and small intestine are lined with microscopic cells that do specialized jobs. Each of these cells is capable of producing a particular enzyme that helps to take apart fat, protein, or carbohydrate.

In addition to the digestive enzymes secreted in the stomach and small intestine, additional enzymes come down through tubes from the pancreas and liver. In other words, the digestion and separation of food particles takes place through the actions of specific enzymes that come first from specialized cells in the stomach, then from cells in the small intestine, and finally from cells in the pancreas and liver. Most of the fat and all of the cholesterol from food pass from the small intestine into the lymphatic system and then into the bloodstream by way of the thoracic duct that opens into the subclavian vein in the left side of the neck. Stated another way, most fatty substances including cholesterol pass through the heart and lungs before reaching the liver. It is in the liver where vitamin B$_6$ is stored in a large quantity. Even more vitamin B$_6$ is stored in the muscles. The liver is a large organ and is loaded with tiny cells that produce the enzymes necessary for life including the proper degradation of food substances.

Specifically, an enzyme is a complex protein produced in a living cell that is able to cause a change in another substance in the body without being changed itself. In other words, enzymes are catalysts. They aid digestion by degrading (taking apart) the protein, carbohydrate, and fat molecules in food. Enzymes are biologic catalysts, sensitive to heat and light, as opposed to inorganic catalysts such as magnesium and calcium, which are not heat or light sensitive.

Vitamin B$_6$, unlike enzymes, is *not* made within the body. Rather, it must be gotten from food. Even cattle and horses depend on food—in their cases, green grass—for their daily intakes of vitamin B$_6$. For people, bananas are a rich source of vitamin B$_6$. Keep in mind, however, that vitamin B$_6$ in food is heat-destructible. A beef roast taken from a hot oven has had 40 percent of its vitamin B$_6$ destroyed. Many bottled, canned, or processed foods have no vitamin B$_6$ at all left in them.

Once vitamin B$_6$ is taken into the body, it goes to work assisting 118 different enzymes in completing their jobs in such tissues as the liver, brain, pancreas, and kidneys. For example, when tryptophan, the most prominent amino acid in beefsteak, enters the bloodstream and is transported to the liver, three little enzymes are lying in wait there to begin the degradation process. These enzymes *require* the assistance of vitamin B$_6$ in taking apart the tryptophan. If vitamin B$_6$ is not present in sufficient quantity, the tryptophan, just partially degraded, becomes toxic, and a deadly disease begins to take hold in the body, in an organ or in the blood. Many top scientists now believe that it is a failure in the precise degradation of tryptophan that leads to changes in the pancreas and causes diabetes. This was first proven to be true in tests done on laboratory rats.

Another amino acid that is present in red meat is methionine. Methionine is degraded by different enzymes than those that take apart tryptophan, but these enzymes, too, require the presence of vitamin B_6 to properly complete their task. Failure in the proper degradation of methionine has been proven to contribute to arteriosclerosis and, therefore, to myocardial infarction.

The process I've been describing is not complicated. It is a part of life, just like breathing oxygen and drinking water. The only difference between metabolism and breathing or drinking is that we can actually see and feel ourselves breathing and drinking, but we can't see and often can't feel the workings inside our bodies. This is why we must trust the many biochemists who have proven in their laboratories that out of the twenty amino acids found in the human body, nineteen require vitamin B_6 for their precise and complete degradation. Thus, we *must* conclude that vitamin B_6 is as important to our healthy survival as are water and air, despite the fact that we cannot see or feel it in action.

The basic way that vitamin B_6 functions in the metabolism of protein from food was summed up as follows by Karl Folkers, Ph.D., a biochemist at the University of Texas in Austin: "Pyridoxine (commonly known as vitamin B_6), pyridoxamine and pyridoxal are the three compounds of the so-called vitamin B_6 group which are widely distributed in nature. The phosphate of pyridoxal is the particularly important coenzyme (pyridoxal-5-phosphate) which is so indispensable and functional in amino acid metabolism."[1] As mentioned previously, the phosphate that is joined to vitamin B_6 is important in protein metabolism, particularly in the kidneys in the excretion of homocysteine.

Vitamin-B_6 deficiency plays a role in a number of disorders and diseases that range from mildly irritating to debilitating.

(For a list of conditions that respond to vitamin-B$_6$ therapy, see page 21.) Primary among these conditions is diabetes. Drs. K.S. Rogers, E.S. Higgins, and E.S. Kline were the first to show that diabetic rats have a lower plasma level than normal rats do. In 1985, they demonstrated that vitamin-B$_6$ deficiency in rats led to an inhibition of the release of insulin from the pancreas. They showed that the kynurenine metabolites—3-hydroxykynurenine, 3-hydroxyanthranilic acid, and 0-aminophenol—inhibited both the glucose- and leucine-stimulated release of insulin from the isolated pancreatic islet of rats. Intravenous (into the vein) administration of these compounds did not alter the plasma levels of insulin in normal rats.[2]

The first association between diabetes and carpal tunnel syndrome was made by Dr. George Phalen. Phalen, a surgeon at the Cleveland Clinic in Cleveland, Ohio, reported that of 103 patients who had surgery for carpal tunnel syndrome, 28 patients, or 27 percent, had either overt diabetes or a history of diabetes in their families.[3] It has been known for a decade that carpal tunnel syndrome is caused by a B$_6$ deficiency. The absence of retinopathy (disorder of the retina) in B$_6$-treated diabetic patients over periods of eight months to twenty-eight years appears monumental. These observations should constitute the basis of a new protocol for establishing the deficiency of vitamin B$_6$ as a molecular cause of diabetic neuropathy (disorder of the nervous system).[4]

In addition to being associated with carpal tunnel syndrome, diabetes is also frequently linked with pregnancy. Over a period of nine years, I treated 225 pregnant women with a daily dosage of 50 to 200 milligrams of vitamin B$_6$, and the carpal tunnel syndrome of 25 of these 225 mothers-to-be was effectively improved.[5,6]

A study that I conducted along with Drs. Karl Folkers, Michael Minadeo, Ronald Van Buskirk, Li-Jun Xia, and Hiroo Tamegawa on diabetes, retinopathy, carpal tunnel syndrome, and vitamin B$_6$ has led to the biochemical and clinical inter-

Conditions That Respond to
Vitamin-B6 Therapy

The following conditions have been shown to respond to treatment with therapeutic doses of vitamin B6:

- ❏ Idiopathic (cause unknown) carpal tunnel syndrome
- ❏ Saccular (sac-like) aneurysm of the aorta
- ❏ Diabetes mellitus
- ❏ Debilitation from cancer caused by nausea, vomiting, and loss of appetite
- ❏ Acute, subacute, and chronic noninflammatory tenosynovitis (inflammation of a tendon sheath due to a biochemical change in the cells rather than pus or a bacterial infection)
- ❏ Acute, subacute, and chronic noninflammatory tendinitis (inflammation of a tendon due to a biochemical change in the cells rather than pus or a bacterial infection)
- ❏ Periarticular synovitis (inflammation of the synovium around multiple joints)
- ❏ DeQuervain's disease (synovitis of the thumb tendons)
- ❏ Shoulder-hand syndrome (severe pain, stiffness, and loss of movement in the entire arm, from the shoulder to the hand and including all the joints in between)
- ❏ Premenstrual edema
- ❏ Menopausal arthritis
- ❏ Pregnancy-related edema
- ❏ Pregnancy-induced hypertension
- ❏ Side effects of the use of birth control pills such as carpal tunnel syndrome and edema
- ❏ Arteriosclerosis

❑ Diabetic retinopathy
❑ Myocardial infarction
❑ Autism in children

Because of the research that is constantly being conducted on vitamin B$_6$, this list is continuing to grow.

pretation that the retinopathy associated with diabetes is the
plausible consequence of a long-standing deficiency of vitamin B$_6$. This interpretation is now the basis of a new protocol
intended to establish whether the retinopathy of diabetes is
indeed a consequence of B$_6$ deficiency, and whether treatment with vitamin B$_6$ can diminish or even eliminate this
retinopathy. The importance of vision justifies the necessity
of giving the benefit of the doubt to this biochemical and clinical interpretation regardless of the strength of the present
evidence.

Not only does vitamin-B$_6$ deficiency contribute to diabetes,
but diabetes contributes to vitamin-B$_6$ deficiency. Specifically,
in humans, elevated blood-glucose levels cause reduced
blood-B$_6$ levels. In other words, a high blood-sugar level contributes to a low blood-B$_6$ level in humans. A study of vita-
min-B$_6$ metabolism in diabetes would be of great significance
because under conditions of high blood sugar, circulating levels of pyridoxal phosphate and total levels of vitamin B$_6$
decrease significantly. On the other hand, B$_6$ deficiency is
known to reduce pancreatic and circulating insulin levels.[7]

Also of importance, homocysteine's documented role as a
risk factor for cardiovascular-disease suggests that a high
plasma level of homocysteine confers an increased risk. The
treatment regimen recommended by Dr. Killian Robinson,
M.D., a cardiologist at the Cleveland Clinic, includes supplemental doses of vitamin B$_6$, vitamin B$_{12}$, and folic acid.[8]

Regarding autism in children, a successful double-blind placebo-controlled crossover study was completed at the University of California. In a double-blind study, neither the subjects nor the researcher know what substance the test group is taking. This allows the researchers to evaluate the results in an unbiased manner. In a crossover study, the subjects take the test substance for a time and then take a blank placebo having no chemical action. In the University of California study, fifteen autistic children were given 300 to 500 milligrams of vitamin B$_6$ and almost 500 milligrams of magnesium daily. Eleven of the children showed positive results, with their thinking and emotional behavior improved. Biochemists have learned that magnesium and vitamin B$_6$ are cofactors in a number of biochemical exchanges. This is especially true in brain function.[9,10]

Other clinicians and scientists have conducted studies on the relationship of magnesium to diabetes. Hypomagnesemia (low blood-magnesium levels) tends to correlate with poor metabolic control, plus appears to be a risk factor for complications such as diabetic retinopathy and ischemic heart disease. The focus has been on magnesium in relationship to the complications of diabetes.[11–13] Evidence now is suggesting that the organically bound forms of chromium—notably chromium picolinate—may indeed promote insulin sensitivity in diabetics. In a double-blind crossover trial using doses providing 200 micrograms of chromium daily, chromium picolinate was found to lower the fasting glucose level by 18 percent and the glycosylated-hemoglobin level by 10 percent. Hemoglobin is the substance in red blood cells that carries oxygen from the lungs to the many tissues in the body. Glycosylated hemoglobin is the particular fraction of red blood cells that has blood sugar attached. Chromium itself does not enter the cells, but assists insulin in getting into them.[14,15]

In effect, in different ways, vitamin B$_6$ is involved with four minerals—chromium and magnesium, as well as zinc and, in presence of diabetes and its associated severe complications, potassium. As a result of inadequate insulin activity and high blood-sugar levels, diabetics have subnormal levels of these minerals. In recent years, biochemists have proven that high blood-sugar levels cause excessive union between glucose and protein in the hemoglobin of blood.[16] In other words, measuring the extent of this union, called the glycohemoglobin level, can help determine what the average blood-sugar level has been during the past one to three months.

The late 1920s represented the heroic age of research into the vitamin-B complex. In addition to discovering vitamin B_6, Dr. Paul György also identified the B complex in general, as well as the antiberiberi factor, vitamin B_1 (thiamine); vitamin B_2 (riboflavin); and biotin, also a B vitamin. A bonus of his work was the recognition of the new vitamins as coenzymes. Dr. György's work was then expanded upon by Dr. Esmond E. Snell, a biochemist at the University of Texas, who was the first to recognize the existence of other forms of vitamin B_6 including pyridoxal and pyridoxamine. Pyridoxine, pyridoxal, and pyridoxamine all owe their B_6 activity to the ability of the organism to convert them through enzymatic pathways (chains of processes) to the coenzyme form, pyridoxal-5-phosphate. To quote A.E. Braunstein, the famous Soviet biochemist, "Pyridoxal phosphate holds an exceptional place among the co-enzymes with regard both to the unparalleled diversity of its catalytic function and to their paramount significance in biochemical transformations of amino acids and in integral pattern of nitrogen metabolism."[17]

Nonscientists must realize that studies of vitamins are tedious and time-consuming. Conclusions are arrived at with great difficulty. Paul György worked twelve years before presenting his first paper on biotin. This is as it should be, for the true scientist is interested, most of all, in what the truth is and what it will mean to the ones who follow him. It is in this spirit that my coauthor and I have written this book. We looked for the *proved* facts that can be depended on as a firm basis for future investigation. The biochemical activities involving vitamin B$_6$ are extremely complex. Where our well-known historical deficiency diseases such as scurvy and beriberi are much easier defined because of their obvious and readily recognizable symptoms, vitamin-B$_6$ deficiency is perceived and described with difficulty. Yet it is probably one of the most rampant deficiency disorders facing this country today. Despite the fact that vitamin B$_6$ is consumed as part of the average daily diet, education is necessary to understand the extent of the body's need and demand for it. This very important vitamin, because of its tendency to be destroyed by heat, will probably be a necessary supplemental vitamin until such time as it is reinstated in processed food products such as wheat flour. The proper and healthy working order of the body depends on vitamin-B$_6$ intake as prescribed in the following chapters.

Chapter 3

THE HISTORY OF VITAMIN B$_6$

L ike an iceberg in foggy, uncharted Antarctic waters, vitamin B$_6$ was hidden for a very long time in scientific obscurity. Even after the laboratory had assigned B$_6$ a valid, but sometimes indefinite, role in human nutrition, the vitamin remained overlooked and undervalued for years. Although vitamin B$_6$ has come a long way from its earliest known role of preventing nutritional dermatitis in rats, it has yet to be fully appreciated by the public for its vital contributions.

The rich history of vitamin B$_6$ stretches back to the dawn of vitamin research, back at least to the first work done with the B-complex vitamins. Its discovery was an offshoot, or windfall, of research aimed at finding other nutrients. The original discovery of a beriberi cure can be traced to 1897 and the work of Dutch physician Christiaan Eykman. Fifteen years later, Casimir Funk separated the antiberiberi factor, which subsequently became known as vitamin B$_1$, or thiamine. He also accomplished another remarkable feat—separating vitamin B$_3$, or nicotinic acid, from unpolished rice. However, he didn't realize that vitamin B$_3$ was the antipellagra factor and thereby postponed its utilization for more than a quarter century. In addition, Funk proposed the "vitamine hypothesis," the idea that the deficiency diseases beriberi and scurvy, and possibly even pellagra and rickets, were caused by the absence of specific chemical substances from the diet. And he coined the name "vitamine," which was later shortened to "vitamin."

Beginning with Funk's discovery of vitamin B_1 in rice polishings, much scientific attention was focused on the treatment and prevention of pellagra, a debilitating disease that ravaged the American South and other poor regions of the world. Vitamin B_6 is in the pathway leading to the formation of vitamin B_3. Vitamin B_3 is the factor that prevents pellagra's "three D's"—diarrhea, dementia, and dermatitis. At the time vitamin B_3 was found to cure pellagra, there were 70,000 new cases a year of the disease in the American South.

In 1915, Dr. Joseph Goldberger became the "pellagra conquest hero." In order to prove pellagra was not contagious, Dr. Goldberger subjected himself and his associates, including his wife, to injections of excrement, nasal mucus, and scale from pellagra sufferers. He, his wife, and his associates all remained free of pellagra, thereby dramatically demonstrating that pellagra is a disease of dietary deficiency.

The scientific world in both Europe and the United States was fermenting during the late 1920s. In 1927, the British Committee on Accessory Food Factors recognized two separate components of the vitamin-B complex—vitamin B_1, the antineuritic, antiberiberi factor, and vitamin B_2, then considered the antipellagra factor and, although it was yet to be isolated, believed to be the only other factor in what is now termed the vitamin-B complex. From the vantage point of time, it is easy to see that the term "vitamin B_2" actually was a large umbrella covering a number of B-complex vitamins. Riboflavin, nicotinic acid, and pyridoxine were all hidden in the jewel case labeled "B_2." Isolating the B vitamins was to be as complicated—and as rewarding—as sorting out rare, twinkling gems from an ancient family treasure chest.

In the late 1920s, Dr. Paul György, a young professor of

pediatrics at Heidelberg University, became interested in the dermatological conditions of infants, a concern that was to lead him down a network of investigatory trails and culminated in his playing a major role in the discoveries of three of the B-complex jewels—vitamin B$_2$, vitamin B$_6$, and biotin. It is interesting to note the international efforts during those fertile years of research. Dr. György himself was on the faculty of three universities in different countries during the period—first, Heidelberg University from 1920 to 1933; then, Cambridge University in England from 1933 to 1935; and, beginning in 1935, Western Reserve University in Cleveland, Ohio, until 1944. By the time he moved to the University of Pennsylvania in 1944, he had completed the bulk of his work on these three vitamins.[1]

When the study of nutrition was in its infancy, the streamlined microbiological tests of today that give results often within hours were only dreams for the distant future. Dr. György, for instance, labored for twelve years before publishing his first scientific paper on biotin.[2] Although a story about vitamin research during those years reads like a roll call of Nobel Prize winners or a Who's Who in Science, funds and assistants were not always easily come by. Research often meant personal involvement of one's family as well. During a 1971 visit of the Györgys to my Texas ranch, Margaret György described those days of the twenties and thirties. "It's not like it used to be," she said. "Back then, I fed the rats for his experiments. Now, they have people who do that."

Essentially, the work to isolate and identify riboflavin took three definite lines of investigation, which broadened out to the discovery of three different vitamins. The first line of investigation involved egg-white injury, a deficiency condition that was produced in rats by limiting the animals' daily protein intake to a ration of dry, uncooked egg white. This raw-egg-white diet caused very severe generalized scaly dermatitis and loss of weight, ending in death. Dr. György worked from 1929 until 1940 to pin down the precise mechanism. Finally, he discovered biotin by proving that something in uncooked egg white bound the nutrient, making it unavailable to the animal. Cooking the egg white unbound the nutrient and allowed it to be absorbed. Dr. György was assisted in his effort by Dr. Vincent du Vigneaud, a professor of biochemistry at Cornell School of Medicine who later, in 1955, won the Nobel Prize in Chemistry for discovering a process for making synthetic hormones. Biotin was subsequently established as important to all living organisms.

Dr. György also visited me in Texas in the spring of 1970. During that visit, I drove him around my ranch, proudly pointing out my Brahman cattle. Stopping in a pasture I had cultivated especially for my herd, I jumped out to pull up a handful of crimson clover plants. I blew off the dirt from the legumes, planning to display them to the distinguished scientist.

"What is he doing?" Dr. György asked my ranch foreman, who had come with us.

"He wants to show you the nodules on the roots of the clover. It's oxygen," the foreman explained just as I hopped back into the car.

"No," I corrected, "it's not oxygen. It's nitrogen in the nodules!"

"Yes. I know," said Dr. György in his fascinating Hungarian accent. "Biotin binds it there."

Along with his other experiments, Dr. György had studied various plants in a home laboratory in his cellar, patiently deepening his understanding of the functions of biotin.

Following his first study—the twelve-year search that ended in the discovery of biotin—Dr. György began his second study. This study grew out of the original dermatological problem and was intended to isolate vitamin B_2, believed at first to be the only other substance in the B-complex family that was not B_1. Dr. György's collaborators in this investigation were two of Europe's leading scientists, Dr. Richard Kuhn and Dr. Theodor Wagner-Jauregg. Dr. Kuhn, of the

Chemistry Department at Heidelberg University, subsequently won the 1938 Nobel Prize in Chemistry for his work on carotenoids and vitamins. Tragically, the Nazis forced him as well as other Germans to decline their Nobel Prizes. Adolf Hitler's anger had been provoked in 1936 when Carl von Ossietzky, an imprisoned pacifist and anti-Nazi, was awarded the Nobel Peace Prize.

The "rat work" on the B$_2$ project involved feeding rats a diet of food prepared free of bacteria and then supplemented with cod-liver oil for vitamins A and D, and an alcoholic extract of the source of vitamin B$_1$. Dr. Wagner-Jauregg, the chemist, separated the various fractions, and Dr. György observed the growth of the rats. The rats were tested over periods of three to four weeks each, a very time-consuming process in comparison to today's often-lightning-quick microbiological tests.

Dr. Wagner-Jauregg prepared a number of concentrates from cow's milk in order to isolate the fractions chemically. Progress was made when he noted that the active concentrates were colored, characterized by a yellowish green fluorescence that varied in intensity in direct proportion to the biological effects. The end of the long search seemed near. As a working hypothesis, Dr. György and his associates identified the long-sought B$_2$ with the yellowish green fluorescence. Accordingly, Dr. Wagner-Jauregg further refined the concentrates until they became more and more colored, greener and greener.

But one day, after carefully observing the rats, Dr. György notified Dr. Wagner-Jauregg that something had gone wrong. The rats were not growing. In the purifying procedure, something essential had been taken out—the vitamin B$_2$ they had been seeking. The yellowish green fluorescence, then, was not what they had been hoping it was. They had been wrong in identifying B$_2$ by color alone. B$_2$ was not green after all. In despair over the failure of the working hypothesis and, it seemed, the entire experiment, Drs. Wagner-Jauregg and

György discussed other possibilities. Dr. György showed that through supplementation with a specially prepared yeast concentrate, the biological activity of the colored preparation could be restored. Dr. Wagner-Jauregg reworked the experiment, backtracking over the just-traveled trail, so to speak, by adding back fractions that had already been eliminated. In this way, vitamin B_2, a pure crystalline yellow compound from milk whey, was isolated by chemists Dr. Kuhn and Dr. Wagner-Jauregg, with Dr. György as a collaborator. The substance was first called "lactoflavin," but later it was given the name "riboflavin."

The discovery of riboflavin was a breakthrough, for the nutrient bridged the gap between cellular metabolism and the essential nutrients (the nutrients required in the diet) and cell enzymes. Riboflavin was the first vitamin to be recognized as part of an enzyme system. This, in biochemical research, represented a special milestone, for since then, the water-soluble vitamins (vitamin C and the B complex) have been found to be *essential* parts of enzyme systems. Ironically, the antipellagra factor, which riboflavin was expected to be, was not yet found. Riboflavin was determined to definitely be an essential vitamin, but it was not found to cure pellagra. The discovery of riboflavin was but another example of the serendipity that would characterize the B-complex research for years. The search for one precious gem instead turned up another, and that other gem led to still another.

The pellagra-preventive (P-P) hunt continued unabated. Dr. György returned to his experimental rats to conduct further feeding experiments. He placed the rats on a diet lacking the vitamin-B complex as a whole, but gave them supplements of thiamine and riboflavin in the recommended amounts. In this way, he could determine if the B family had other essential members. After a few weeks on this diet, the young rats showed reduced growth rates and developed scaly sores, most pronounced on their peripheral body parts such as the tail, paws, ears, and snout. Accompanying edema (swelling of the structures affected with sores) was of great importance in distinguishing the disorder from dermatitis caused by a diet deficient in certain polyunsaturated fats. Since the cutaneous lesions somewhat resembled those found on humans suffering from pellagra, Dr. György called the induced condition in the rats "pellagra-like," but "without prejudice as to their identity or nonidentity with human pellagra." Thus, Dr. György established that vitamin B_2 was not a single vitamin, but a complex in itself.

At the time, other investigators had already claimed the names B_3, B_4, B_5, and even Y for substances they believed to be vitamins. Therefore, Dr. György skipped these labels and called his "rat-pellagra-preventive" vitamin B_6. Eventually, vitamin B_3 was proven to be the pellagra-preventive and was later relabeled nicotinic acid, or niacin. Vitamins B_4 and B_5 were found not to be vitamins at all but other substances, which is why at present there are no such vitamins.

Although vitamin B_6 had finally been found, much hard work remained to be done to prove that it actually existed as a separate nutrient. For the next two years, from 1935 to 1937, investigations by a number of scientists established the distinctions between riboflavin, nicotinic acid, and B_6—in Dr. György's words, "the separate existence of these three members of the vitamin B complex." In 1937, Dr. Conrad A. Elvehjem, an instructor at the Agricultural College of the University of Wisconsin, determined that nicotinic acid was the P-P factor that researchers had been intensively seeking. One result of this was that the designation of B_6-deficiency as "pellagra-like dermatitis" was changed to "rat acrodynia," but without any reference to human acrodynia. The next step was to isolate the pure crystalline vitamin B_6, and Dr. György was but one of many who strenuously labored to do this. When I visited San Francisco in 1972, I had the privilege of discussing this period of discovery with Dr. Samuel Lepkovsky, one of the other scientists involved in the search. Dr. Lepkovsky, Polish-born like his friend Dr. Funk, came to the United States with his parents when he was six years old. As he and I discussed the earlier period, he recalled Dr. György's preparing a crude fraction containing the nutrient that would relieve rat acrodynia. Other "contenders in the race" were Dr. Kuhn, Dr. György's former associate, now with the I.G. Farben Company in Germany; Stanton A. Harris and Karl Folkers of Merck and Company in this country; and Dr. Lepkovsky, the dark horse.

In early 1938, several of the investigators had the goal in sight. In a warm gesture not often experienced in the highly competitive world of scientific research, Dr. Lepkovsky, when he finished isolating the pure compound, wrote to Dr. György and urged him to submit his paper for publication as soon as possible. He advised Dr. György that he as well as another scientist, J.C. Keresztesy, were both ready to submit their own papers. This enabled Dr. György, now aware of the urgency, to submit his paper in time. Lepkovsky's gesture was one that Dr. György never forgot. "Research by itself," Dr. Lepkovsky said to me in 1972, "is worthwhile without seeking the honor of who is first." This is something I will never forget.

Dr. Lepkovsky, then, was the first to report the isolation of pure crystalline B_6—from liver and yeast—in an article in the American journal *Science* in 1938, just four years after the nutrient's discovery by Dr. György. Slightly later that same year, other researchers, including Dr. György, reported its isolation independently of Dr. Lepkovsky, in American, German, and Japanese scientific journals. Within a year, American researchers Stanton A. Harris and Karl Folkers of Merck and Company's research laboratory, writing in the *Journal of the American Chemical Society*, and Germans Richard Kuhn, K. Westphal, G. Wendt, and O. Westphal, writing in *Naturwissenschaften*, made clear the exact chemical structure of vitamin B_6—a pyridine ring. (See Figure 3.1.) Because of this chemical structure, Dr. György proposed the name "pyridoxine" for the compound.

As the father of vitamin B$_6$, Paul György discovered it, independently isolated it, and named it, thus closing out what he was later to classify as "one of the most intriguing chapters in the rapid development of vitamin research."[3] Thereafter, the nutrient had his stamp on it, although scores of other researchers were connected to it intimately because of their own contributions. However, immediately after its discovery, isolation, and synthesis, vitamin B$_6$ was in the curious position of being, at least temporarily, a glamour vitamin, with its proven usefulness limited to the relief of rat acrodynia. And although some brief clinical work was done with it, the vitamin essentially kept this reputation for more than a decade.

But the clinical work appeared promising. By June 10, 1939, less than two months after its synthesis, vitamin B$_6$ made the news once again, this time via an article in the *Journal of the American Medical Association* written by three doctors in Birmingham, Alabama, who reported what apparently was the nutrient's first human use. The doctors—Tom Douglas Spies, another pioneer in the pellagra war; William B. Bean; and William F. Ashe—announced the dramatic, twenty-four-hour recoveries of four patients who were treated with pure vitamin B$_6$ at Hillman Hospital in Birmingham. Earlier, the patients had been treated for pellagra and beriberi, caused

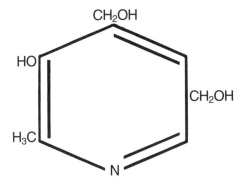

Figure 3.1. Since the chemical structure of vitamin B$_6$ is a pyridine ring, Dr. Paul György proposed the name "pyridoxine" for the compound.

by, respectively, deficiencies of niacin and thiamine. After their recoveries, the patients had returned to their inadequate diets and again developed their old symptoms. This time, though, they were each given 50 milligrams of pure synthetic vitamin B$_6$. Both the doctors and the patients were astounded when all the symptoms disappeared within twenty-four hours. Before treatment, one man had been unable to walk more than a few steps. The day after he was injected with B$_6$, he walked two miles without fatigue![4]

Dr. Spies, who later, near the end of his career, received the Distinguished Service Award of the American Medical Association, was a clinical pioneer in treating pellagra and other deficiency diseases following the discovery and synthesis of vitamin B$_3$ as the pellagra preventive. In 1940, Dr. Spies reported additional remarkable changes effected by B$_6$ therapy. Speaking at the 100th Annual Meeting of the Illinois State Medical Society, he described patients suffering from Parkinson's disease who responded within a few minutes of intravenous injection with B$_6$.

Parkinson's disease, a shaking palsy marked by muscular weakness, stiffness, and pain, was a severe and lingering disease that had hitherto been considered more or less hopeless. Dr. Spies and his associate, Dr. Bean, had treated eleven cases of Parkinsonism that had existed for at least four years. Eight of the patients were arteriosclerotic, and three were post-encephalitic. The best results came with the three patients who had had encephalitis. These patients had shown improvement a few minutes after injection. Their tremors and rigidity had decreased enough so that they could walk without the customary stiffness. Two of the arteriosclerotic patients also showed definite improvement, but five were unchanged and one was considerably worse. Dr. Spies additionally reported that similar results with Parkinsonism patients had been communicated to him by Dr. Norman H. Jolliffe of the New York University College of Medicine.[5] All of these reports, however, were soon forgotten, never followed up with any widespread, intensive clinical activity related to B_6.

It was at this point, when clinical interest seemed to be fading, that microbiological research entered the picture. In 1942, a brilliant biochemist at the University of Texas, Dr. Esmond E. Snell, still in his twenties, established the existence of two other forms of vitamin B_6—pyridoxal and pyridoxamine. Dr. Snell found that the three forms exist in nature, and that there is a difference in the rate of growth of certain bacteria depending on which one of the three forms is present. He also proved that, once taken into the human body, all three forms combine with phosphate to form pyridoxal phosphate, which is the reactive principle of B_6. It is this coenzyme that speeds up and stimulates the necessary biochemical reactions in human metabolism.

Thus, vitamin B_6 became known as a subgroup of the vitamin-B_2 complex, with pyridoxine, pyridoxal, and pyridoxamine as its particular chemical representatives. Subsequently, B_6 was found to be distributed widely in both animal and plant products, usually as pyridoxine in plants and seeds, and as pyridoxal and pyridoxamine in animal products. It is most abundant in whole-grain cereals, fish, milk, eggs, vegetables, and yeast. While pyridoxine remains stable when heated, pyridoxal and pyridoxamine can be partially destroyed by cooking, and all forms are sensitive to light and vigorous oxidation. In fact, all of the B vitamins are water-soluble, and the longer green vegetables are boiled, the less food value they have. Among the B_6-rich foods that can be eaten uncooked are brewer's yeast, wheat germ, bananas, pecans, and avocados. According to chemical analysis, bananas are about five times richer in vitamin B_6 than any other fruit.

Close on the heels of Dr. Snell, Samuel Lepkovsky and associates, working at the University of California at Berkeley and the California Institute of Technology at Pasadena, reported in 1943 the isolation of xanthurenic acid from the urine of pyridoxine-deficient rats. They showed that xanthurenic acid was an abnormal metabolite of the amino acid tryptophan and related to vitamin-B_6 deficiency. When pyridoxine was added to the diet, xanthurenic acid immediately disappeared from the urine. Thus, xanthurenic acid was recognized as an indicator of metabolic derangement as the result of inadequate pyridoxine levels.[6] This led to the development of a valuable diagnostic tool that was to see extensive use in the years ahead—the tryptophan load test. If tryptophan is not metabolized normally, xanthurenic acid will be excreted in the urine. Following the work of Dr. Lepkovsky's group, the test became common for determining the B_6 level in both humans and experimental animals.[7]

In the years that followed, despite the laboratory findings and Dr. Spies' work with humans, vitamin B_6 seemed to go through a period of the doldrums, with few uses found for it clinically. In the words of Dr. György, "With all the rich history of vitamin B_6, approximately twenty years passed before its requirement by the human organism had been definitely established and recognized."[8] One of the reasons for this was the disrupting effect of World War II, which conscripted the energies and talents of scientists around the world and kept doctors overworked merely taking care of patients. When the war was over, medical interest focused on other, more glamorous fields. Vitamin B_6 was left by the wayside as new wonder drugs competed for the spotlight.

However, in 1952, evidence finally emerged that B_6 was essential to humans. That year, a commercial milk formula caused convulsions in infants. It was subsequently proven that the excessive heating of the formula during processing caused the naturally occurring vitamin B_6 to be destroyed to such a point that the resulting deficiency of the nutrient in infants caused serious impairment in brain function. The story began in the town of Harrison, Arkansas, a little county seat in the Ozarks. A mother telephoned Dr. William P. Barron for help with her convulsing baby. The baby, shaking all over, had turned blue. Dr. Barron rushed to the home and methodically examined the baby, but found no evidence of serious disease. He hospitalized the baby and ordered all the diagnostic tests that might cast light—X-ray, blood, urine, and spinal-fluid studies. All the tests came back with negative results, indicating that the baby was healthy. But the convulsions continued.

In the hospital, the baby was fed a whole-milk-and-sugar formula instead of the commercial formula he had been getting. By the third day of hospitalization, the baby had but one seizure. By the fourth day, his convulsions had ended. What had changed to improve the condition? There seemed to be no clues, nothing to go on. But soon, as similar cases came into that and other hospitals, a pattern began to appear. The babies were mainly from four to sixteen weeks old, they were convulsing, and they were on the same commercial formula. When the formula was changed, the convulsions disappeared. Dr. Barron and others, including Dr. B.P. Briggs of Little Rock and Dr. J.O. Cooper of El Dorado, reported their observations to the Arkansas State Health Department in Little Rock.

Although cases were reported in various parts of the country, a concentration of them was channeled to the Arkansas State Health Department, where the milk formula had become suspect. By May 12, 1953, the matter had reached the AMA's Council on Foods and Nutrition, which sought details from the University of Arkansas School of Medicine in Little Rock. Dr. Katharine Dodd, professor of pediatrics, personally went through the records of the cases handled at the School of Medicine, copied them over in longhand, and dispatched the copies to Chicago. At the same time, Dr. Johan Eliot, pediatric consultant to the Arkansas State Health Department and one of the first to suspect a connection between the formula and the convulsions, sent the AMA the records he had collected in Texas and Arkansas. Further evidence was contributed by Dr. David B. Coursin of Lancaster, Pennsylvania.

Within forty-eight hours, the AMA council had collected enough evidence to definitely implicate the formula. The manufacturer was notified and voluntarily took the formula off the market. By May 22, all of the milk had been removed from all the stores in the United States that carried it.[9] The flaw in the formula was traced to changes the company had made in the product some time earlier. A different type of fat was used, and the formula was heated more than previously. Later, the excessive heating was pinpointed as the cause of problem.

Years later, I discussed this medical mystery with L.J. Filer, M.D., Ph.D., professor of pediatrics at the University of Iowa School of Medicine. Dr. Filer said that because of work he had done with rats, he had suspected that the convulsions were caused by inadequate B_6. As a result, he did an assay on the milk. Dr. Coursin, director of research at St. Joseph's Hospital in Lancaster, Pennsylvania, then did an electroencephalogram on a baby having convulsions and proved that B_6 injections stopped the convulsions and prevented further ones. Thus, it was determined that naturally occurring B_6 could be destroyed by heat to a point where the resulting dietary deficiency caused serious impairment in brain function.

In other hospitals and clinics, connections between additional disorders and vitamin B_6 were subsequently determined. For example, it was learned that B_6 relieves neuritis in the arms, legs, hands, and feet of tuberculosis patients treated with certain medications. These medications include the tuberculosis drug isoniazid, found to induce a B_6 deficiency by combining with the active form of the vitamin, pyridoxal phosphate, and causing it to be eliminated in the urine.[10] For this reason, tuberculosis sanitariums began using large amounts of B_6 to counteract the destruction of the vitamin by the drug antagonists.

Other investigators found a relationship between an increased need for B_6 and Down syndrome, a congenital disorder marked by a mild to moderate failure of normal mental development. Convulsive seizures in children who were mentally retarded could be eliminated by increased amounts of B_6. Radiologists used B_6 in an effort to relieve to a limited extent the nausea associated with deep-X-ray treatment for cancer, while obstetricians claimed some success in treating the nausea of pregnancy. Other physicians found the vitamin useful in relieving a rare type of anemia, not the normal iron-deficiency anemia, but one marked by unusually small red blood cells and apparently the result of a defective hereditary factor responsive to B$_6$.[11] However, in an unsuccessful clinical experience, it was found that a peculiar type of photosensitivity, a rare condition characterized by intolerance to sunlight and severe sunburn after very little exposure, was made worse when vitamin B$_6$ was given.

Summarizing the work of these decades, Paul György wrote that "the history of vitamin B$_6$ is a further proof that success usually is preceded by trials, tribulations, and recurrent disappointment. The most helpful factor, apart from perseverance and timeliness of the line of research, is the deliberate recognition of a principle that is paramount in scientific research; it is often almost beyond our control, and touches closely on intuition. It is Walter B. Cannon's 'serendipity.'"[12]

This is an apt characterization of B$_6$ history. And on the basis of my own experiences with the vitamin, I would also agree with a *Journal of the American Medical Association* editorial, though written on another subject, stating that "apparently, unlike lightning, serendipity can strike more than once in the same place, and, as distinct from the former, it illuminates without destroying."[13]

This, basically, was the sum of the rich history of vitamin B$_6$ when I first became interested in the nutrient in 1961. Needless to say, I was not then aware of what I have written in this chapter. I had not read about the vitamin to any extent, nor did I know anything about the early clinical work of Dr. Spies. Although evidence about the dangers of vitamin-B$_6$ deficiency was already building in the laboratory, the problems caused by lack of the nutrient were not common knowledge among doctors and, in 1961, vitamin-B$_6$ deficiency was even believed overwhelmingly not to exist in the United States.

Prior to 1961, it appeared that vitamin B_6 only helped humans with rare and unusual disease conditions, such as infants suffering convulsions from the use of a defective milk formula and tuberculosis patients with peripheral neuritis from treatment with drug antagonists. Today, through my studies, I know of eighteen conditions that respond to vitamin-B_6 therapy. (For the list, see "Conditions That Respond to Vitamin-B_6 Therapy" on page 21.) Through the same studies, I have collected a detailed list of the signs and symptoms associated with vitamin-B_6 deficiency. (For this list, see "Signs and Symptoms of Vitamin-B_6 Deficiency in the Human Body" on page 43.) But even with all the research and clinical data now available on B_6 therapies, the scientific community is slow to respond. I remember talking with two of the best chemists in the world, and after discussing my findings, one looked at the other and said, "If only we could believe half of what he says to be true." It was a frustrating experience for me.[14]

I recently wrote the following introduction and attached it to an investigative report concerning the treatment of coronary heart disease with vitamin B_6:

Regarding the treatment of coronary heart disease with vitamin B_6, some review of the literature is necessary. The pathogenesis of experimental arteriosclerosis in vitamin B_6 deficiency was first reported in 1951.[15] Occlusive vascular pathology [manifestation of disease] was subsequently demonstrated in association with high plasma level of homocysteine that to a degree is favorably controlled by adequate vitamin B_6.[16] Vitamin B_6 deficiency associated with carpal tunnel syndrome was determined in the laboratory based on a cross-over clinical study.[17] A summary of successful treatment of carpal tunnel syndrome in the hands of 11 percent of 225 pregnant women was described at conclusion of nine years of study.[18,19] Plasma homocysteine was found to be a risk factor for myocar-

Signs and Symptoms of Vitamin-B$_6$ Deficiency in the Human Body

The following signs and symptoms signal a possible vitamin-B$_6$ deficiency:

❑ Paresthesia (pins and needles numbness and tingling in distal parts of the hands or feet) in the hands
❑ Impaired sensation in the fingers
❑ Impaired flexion of the finger joints
❑ Fluctuating edema in the hands
❑ Morning stiffness in the finger joints
❑ Pain in the hands
❑ Impaired coordination of the fingers
❑ Weakness of pinch (the pressure between the thumb and index finger)
❑ Increased tendency to drop objects
❑ Tenderness over the carpal tunnel with Tinel's sign (a tingling sensation radiating out into the hand and accompanied by pain at the wrist) and Phalen's sign (paresthesia in the fingers that becomes worse when the median nerve is squeezed between the ligament and tendons while the wrist is held flexed for thirty to sixty seconds)
❑ Pain in the shoulders
❑ Pain upon movement of the thumb knuckle (metacarpophalangeal joint)
❑ Pain in the elbows
❑ Sleep paralysis (the temporary inability to lift the arm or hand upon awakening during the night)
❑ Edema from steroid-hormone therapy (a puffy swelling in the tissues of the face, hands, feet, or legs when

steroid hormones, particularly large doses of cortisone or female hormones such as estrogen, are taken)
❏ Macular edema (an abnormal collection of fluid and fatty substances that have leaked from tiny arteries near the central portion of the retina of the eye, resulting in disturbed central vision)

If you notice any of these signs and symptoms, contact your physician. You may find vitamin-B₆ therapy to be extremely helpful.

dial infarction in U.S. physicians.[20] Cardiologists concluded that hyperhomocysteinemia and low pyridoxal phosphate are common and independent reversible risk factors for coronary artery disease.[21] Evidence was presented that vitamin B₆ in doses of 200–300 mg/day [milligrams per day] prevented macular edema leading to retinopathy and blindness in patients having diabetes mellitus. Grouped in a physiological state were pregnancy, carpal tunnel syndrome and retinopathy leading to diabetic blindness.[22] In a mini-review, vitamin B₆ metabolism has been correlated with diabetes.[23] Extensive clinical and epidemiological research in Northeast Texas leads to the conclusion that myocardial infarction is preventable with vitamin B₆ therapy.[24]

These amazing scientific articles recently published in prestigious journals of medicine and science constitute discovery that leads to future treatment and prevention of deadly, crippling, and blinding disease conditions caused by vitamin B₆ deficiency. This is fantastic information important to millions of people.

Each sentence in this introduction material is referenced, and although being far from comprehensive concerning the benefits of vitamin B$_6$, this introduction to the report on coronary heart disease should give you some idea of the studies that have been conducted and of the remarkable future potential of vitamin-B$_6$ therapy.

Chapter 4

CARPAL TUNNEL SYNDROME

You're behind a desk, typing on a computer keyboard for up to eight hours a day, five days a week. So far, you've been lucky—your wrists still work. They don't hurt when you lift your hand into position. But one out of every ten Americans with a repetitive-type job isn't so lucky.

In 1990, carpal tunnel syndrome and related repetitive-motion injuries cost American businesses twenty billion dollars. Affected workers were either temporarily or permanently disabled, and many were caught up in the frenzy of personal-injury liability and litigation. Corporations and even small businesses responded with better equipment, mainly because the real answer to the problem sounded just too simple. What court would give a business consideration if all it did to correct the problem was tell its suffering employees to take vitamin B_6 and get back to work. Yet, in nearly all cases, vitamin B_6 is the most important component in the treatment of carpal tunnel syndrome. In fact, adequate dietary intake of B_6 is also the most important element in avoiding the development of the disease.[1]

Carpal tunnel syndrome includes all the conditions that produce irritation or compression of the median nerve within the carpal tunnel. The syndrome occurs when the median nerve that runs through the carpal-tunnel opening in the wrist gets pinched or pressured from constant redundant motions. The result is similar to what happens when you pinch a drinking straw. The median nerve is the major pathway for the nerve impulses coming from the spinal cord. (See Figure 4.1.) These nerve impulses travel down the arm through the wrist and palm into the fingers. The median nerve supplies most of the sensation to the hand and muscle power to the thumb.

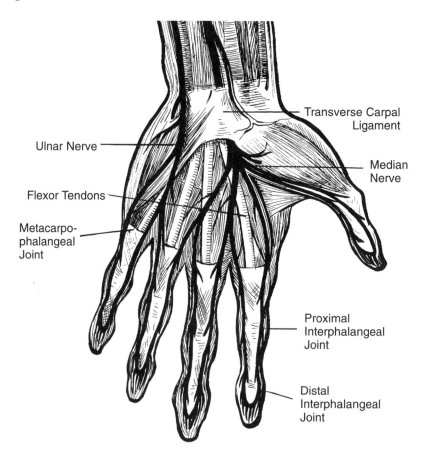

Figure 4.1. Diagram of a hand, palm-side up. Note how the median nerve goes to the thumb and the index, middle, and ring fingers, and a separate nerve, called the ulnar nerve, goes to the little finger.

Ordinarily, bones and ligaments form a protective tunnel of sorts around the median nerve and tendons in the wrist. But if something goes haywire—for example, from that last hit of a key, turn of a switch, thrust of a needle, or lift of a tray—the protective tunnel may fail and allow the median nerve to become pinched. There does not have to be, and in most cases there is not, a history of wrist injury. The disease can hit suddenly or creep up on you, affecting one or both hands. But once the normal flow of nutrients to the median nerve is disrupted, short-circuiting nerve impulses will soon drive you to a doctor's office. If treatment is delayed, the problem can eventually cause your thumb, index finger, and middle-finger to starve, and the thumb muscles to atrophy and become useless.[2,3]

Although the standard medical therapies of cortisone injections and surgery can be effective in the treatment of carpal tunnel syndrome, they sometimes leave sufferers with a degree of disability, along with an unaddressed vitamin-B_6 deficiency. In a 1990 clinical test, Dr. Karl Folkers and I worked with twenty-two cases of carpal tunnel syndrome, some complicated because the patient had already had surgery for the problem. A dose of 50 to 300 milligrams of vitamin B_6 every day for twelve weeks brought relief to all but one of the affected thirty-nine hands. This is a cure rate of 97.4 percent, a figure higher than what is usually achieved by surgery alone.

Dr. Folkers and I noted subjective changes in pain, paresthesia, and tactile sensation in the study participants. Our proof of change was objective—namely, we measured the flexion in the index finger with a goniometer, and determined the weakness in the thumb as pounds pinch with a Preston Pinch Gauge. (See Figure 4.2.) In cases caught early, the twelve weeks of 50 to 300 milligrams of vitamin B_6 daily also prevented the occurrence of atrophy in the thenar (palm) muscle. In other words, the vitamin B_6 prevented loss in the size and function of the two muscles at the base of the thumb. In the cases of bilateral carpal tunnel syndrome in which

Figure 4.2.
The Preston Pinch
Gauge measures
the strength in the
fingers—specifically the
index finger and thumb.

surgery had been performed on one hand and vitamin B_6 was begun following the surgery, the patients invariably stated that after the twelve weeks of vitamin therapy, the hand that was not surgically treated "got well" anyway.

The biochemical evidence supporting the findings of this twenty-two-patient study showed that those patients with severe carpal tunnel syndrome and a significant deficiency of vitamin B_6 had extraordinarily low basal-specific activity of erythrocyte glutamic-oxaloacetic transaminase (EGOT). Dr. Folkers and other chemists at the University of Texas in Austin had demonstrated a close relationship between the vitamin-B_6 blood level and EGOT activity. Patients with the lowest activity had severe symptoms of proven vitamin-B_6 deficiency. This allowed correlation and diagnosis of vitamin-B_6 deficiency.

Altogether, sixty-one monitorial assays of EGOT were done on the twenty-two patients over a forty-eight-week period. The results of the assays supported the following interpretations:

❏ The patients' diets permitted the development of debilitating carpal tunnel syndrome.

❏ Treatment with vitamin B_6 at a dosage of 2 milligrams per day (the RDA of vitamin B_6) for eleven weeks reduced the deficiency of EGOT from about 70 percent to 50 percent, maintained the deficiency of pyridoxal phosphate, and relieved but allowed marginal carpal tunnel syndrome.

❏ Treatment with vitamin B_6 at a dosage of 100 milligrams per day for twelve weeks nearly achieved a ceiling level of EGOT and eliminated the deficiency of pyridoxal phosphate.

❏ Treatment with a placebo (unknown to the patient) for seven weeks allowed the deficiencies of EGOT activity and pyridoxal phosphate to reappear and the clinical symptoms of carpal tunnel syndrome to become worse.

❏ Re-treatment with vitamin B_6 at a dosage of 100 milligrams per day reestablished the ceiling level of EGOT and eliminated the pyridoxal-phosphate deficiency and carpal-tunnel-syndrome symptoms.

Finally, two orthopedic surgeons independently concluded that "surgery of the carpal tunnel was unnecessary."[4]

Vitamin B_6 works by improving the function of the synovium, the sheath that surrounds the tendons. The vitamin also helps to stimulate the body's production of cortisone, which in turn reduces the swelling in the tendons compressing the median nerve.[5,6] (See Figure 4.3.) B_6 is essential to the maintenance of hyaluronic acid, the lubricant inside the carpal tunnel and between the joints. It is also essential for the body's healthy production of adrenaline.[7,8]

Unfortunately, the constant low level of anxiety prevalent in modern society keeps the adrenaline pumping continually, depleting the body's meager store of vitamin B_6 much faster than normal. This increased adrenaline flow negatively stimulates the liver into processing lactic acid back into blood glucose at a faster rate. The buildup of lactic acid in the mus-

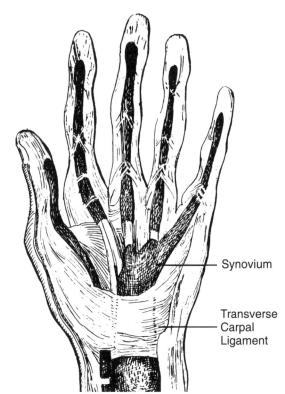

Figure 4.3.
In carpal tunnel
syndrome, the
synovium swells and
becomes trapped
beneath the trans-
verse carpal ligament,
causing pressure on
the median nerve
and intense pain and
numbness in the
thumb, index finger,
and middle finger.

Synovium

Transverse
Carpal
Ligament

cles of the forearm produces fatigue, slows down repetitive motions, and increases injury potential.[9] Thus, the number of carpal-tunnel-syndrome cases rises along with workplace stress factors and the increase in computer and other repetitive-motion jobs.

My first formal paper linking carpal tunnel syndrome and vitamin-B$_6$ deficiency appeared in the Winter 1972 edition of the *Journal of Applied Nutrition*. I presented two case histories to identify carpal tunnel syndrome and its response to supplemental vitamin B$_6$. One of the case histories was of a thirty-three-year-old clerk-typist whose right hand had become weak about ten days prior to coming to see me. Her left hand was not affected.

"If I try to pick something up," the clerk-typist had said, "I nearly drop it. This past week, I could not move my thumb toward my other fingers enough to hold my pen. Once in a while, I have a spasm in my fingers and have to pull or massage them to get them to function again. For the past month, my right hand has awakened me at night. My hand would feel numb and asleep, and it was painful. I could get some relief by hanging it over the side of the bed. Sometimes my fingers would seem swelled, and my birthstone ring would be tight. My right thumb now feels weak, and the thumb joint [the metacarpophalangeal joint of the thumb] feels like it is out of place when I move my thumb."

An examination of the patient proved that pain in the right hand resulted when pressure was applied to the palm side of the wrist, with the pain radiating up the arm for ten centimeters. There was also slight edema of the right hand, cold perspiration on the skin of the palm, and weakness of the abductor muscles (the muscles that move the thumb away from the hand) of the right thumb. The uric-acid level was normal, the urine was negative for sugar and albumin, and the hemoglobin level was 14.4, all of which indicated this patient had normal kidney function without diabetes. The patient had taken an anti-ovulatory contraceptive pill for ten years, but during the past six years, she had taken no vitamin supplement of any kind.

I began my treatment of the clerk-typist with an intravenous injection of the vitamin-B complex including 50 milligrams of vitamin B_6. In addition, I prescribed 50 milligrams of vitamin B_6 by mouth morning and night. Three days later, the patient exhibited a reduction in the edema, and she could remove her birthstone ring with ease. The numbness and tingling had subsided, and all the pain in the hand and lower forearm was gone. A week later, the patient stated, "For a month and a half before taking vitamin B_6, I could not grip a skillet to lift it from the stove. Today, I lifted the skillet without any reservation."

The second case history I described in my *Journal of Applied Nutrition* article was that of a twenty-one-year-old pregnant woman. The young mother-to-be's family history included a deceased diabetic grandfather, an aunt suffering from acroparesthesia (numbness, edema, and inability to bend the fingertips toward the palms), and a brother who had Down syndrome. The patient herself had edema in her hands and feet. I prescribed a daily prenatal multi-vitamin-and-mineral supplement and an additional 50 milligrams of vitamin B_6.

In response to the vitamin therapy, the edema subsided. However, it reappeared one month later. I increased the vitamin-B_6 dosage to 110 milligrams, and within one week, the edema was again gone. But the edema came back once more, and once again I increased the vitamin-B_6 dosage. Upon hospital admission in labor, after having received 310 milligrams of vitamin B_6 daily for the last thirty days of her pregnancy, the patient exhibited no edema. Because of a breech presentation of the fetus, a cesarean section was performed, but neither the mother nor the infant experienced any complications.

I also treated the aunt who suffered from acroparesthesia. A dosage of 50 milligrams of vitamin B_6 daily brought her complete relief from the pain in her shoulders, arms, and hands.[10]

All subsequent crossover and double-blind studies have demonstrated positively that 100 to 300 milligrams of vitamin B_6 taken daily by mouth relieves the severe signs and symptoms of carpal tunnel syndrome.[11,12] In my own clinical studies, spanning over thirty years, vitamin B_6 was an effective treatment for carpal tunnel syndrome in all but five cases. Those five patients needed surgery to remove ligament in the carpal tunnel to relieve pressure on the nerve and prevent permanent disability.[13]

Carpal tunnel syndrome is really nothing new. As early as 1880, intense numbness in the hands from the wrists down was described by Dr. James Jackson Putnam, a Harvard Medical School professor writing in the *Archives of Medicine*.[14] A similar description of paresthesia was named "acroparesthesia" by German researcher and physician F. Schultze in 1893.[15]

In a special review of carpal tunnel syndrome, N. Taylor stated that although the description of the syndrome has evolved over nearly a century, it was listed as a disease entity by the *Index Medicus* beginning only in 1965.[16]

Drs. B.W. Cannon and J.G. Love are credited with sectioning the transverse carpal ligament in 1946 to relieve pressure on the median nerve,[17] and W.R. Brain, A.D. Wright, and M. Wilkerson in 1947 reported surgical treatment of spontaneous compression of the median nerve by sectioning the transverse carpal ligament.[18] This spontaneous compression of the median nerve eventually became known as carpal tunnel syndrome.

One investigator, Dr. George Phalen, a surgeon at the Cleveland Clinic for twenty-five years and an authority in the field, gave monumental descriptions of 439 patients treated for carpal tunnel syndrome beginning in 1947. He found the synovium covering the flexor tendons of the fingers to be thickened and edematous in many of these cases. He attributed the varying degrees of weakness in the hands to atrophy of the median nerve. He correctly pointed to diabetes as a disease condition associated with carpal tunnel syndrome and also noted an affiliation between the disease and women, at a ratio of three to one over men. Many of the women were near the age of menopause, which suggested a hormonal relationship. Other systemic disorders indicative of hormonal imbalance associated with carpal tunnel syndrome were myxedema (low thyroid secretion) and acromegaly (increase in the size of the hands, feet, and face because of an overproduction of growth hormone due to a tumor on the pituitary gland). Other disease conditions that he found rather frequently were trigger finger or thumb, rheumatoid arthritis, periarthritis of the shoulder, and tennis elbow.[19–25]

A relationship between a derangement in hormone metabolism and carpal tunnel syndrome can be seen again with the use of anti-ovulatory contraceptive pills. The simulated state of pregnancy brought on by the pills results in a B_6 deficiency, the same way actual pregnancy does. This has been confirmed in the laboratory by A.L. Luhby and his associates, who concluded that up to 30 milligrams of vitamin B$_6$ are needed daily to normalize the excretion of urinary metabolites by women who use contraceptive pills.[26–28] Both pregnant women and women on the pill therefore should automatically take vitamin-B$_6$ supplements.

Y. Kotake, Jr., has discovered through animal research that xanthurenic acid, found in increased levels in the presence of B$_6$ deficiency, can cause diabetes.[29–31] Eclampsia is far more common in diabetic pregnant women than in nondiabetic pregnant women.

True carpal tunnel syndrome caused by vitamin-B$_6$ deficiency can appear in conjunction with pregnancy, diabetes, the use of birth control pills, and the continued use of steroid hormones including estrogen and cortisone. However, because the signs and symptoms of carpal tunnel syndrome are the same as those for lupus erythematosis, rheumatoid arthritis, myxedema, and injuries at the wrist from fractures, sprains, and excessive repetitive motion, medical and surgical considerations should be closely evaluated.

It takes thirty days of treatment with 200 milligrams of vitamin B$_6$ daily to get the affected enzymes back up to maximum activity, and it takes sixty more days of treatment with 200 milligrams of vitamin B$_6$ daily to bring relief from true carpal tunnel syndrome. In effect, this means that all patients with the signs and symptoms of carpal tunnel syndrome must begin treatment with vitamin B$_6$ at a daily dose of 200 milligrams as soon as they first feel the numbness, tingling, and pain in their hands. If, after ninety days, the numbness, tingling, and pain persist, the other disease conditions or injuries should be considered, diagnosed, and treated medically or surgically.

Chapter 5

GYNECOLOGIC AND OBSTETRIC DISORDERS

A century ago, in the dark of the night, John Riley Ellis rolled out of bed in his home in the uplands south of the White Oak bottom in eastern Texas. A man was calling out for help. "My wife is sick," the man said, and explained that after having given birth to a baby one week earlier, his wife was suffering from swelling and pain in one of her breasts. Some older women might say that "she had a 'weed' in her breast."

A "saddlebag doctor" might have treated this inflammation and bacterial infection that could lead to abscess by lancing the breast, perhaps a number of times. My grandfather went to the beehive beneath the old pear tree and carved out a section of honeycomb. He instructed the young husband to warm the waxy honeycomb and apply it to the bare skin of the new mother's breast for an indefinite period. This was the accepted cure at the time. The activities of the powerful female sex hormones, tissue changes, lactation, and proper nutrition during pregnancy were then unknown.[1]

Even today, animal-husbandry knowledge outranks personal-body knowledge. Farmers know that if a cow doesn't give one to two gallons of milk a day, her calf will experience

retarded growth. Cowboys know that riding a bronco mare
during her estrous cycle, or a stallion in the presence of such
a mare, will take a heavy controlling hand, or the resulting
rough ride may send the rider skyward. Humans have no
estrous cycle, but they do have the same sex hormones, hormones that send both female and male reeling down the aisle
of love. Unlike animals, however, a bride, radiant and beautiful, and a groom, knees trembling, can express both hormonal and emotional control, which ultimately promote
well-being. But without a working knowledge of the mysteries supporting life and an understanding of what it takes to
sustain health, humans are just as likely to fall into emotional and physical disrepair as any unattended animal. What
herdsman would dare feed his animals a diet lacking the
essential nutrients and still expect to make a healthy profit?
Yet each day, that same herdsman may sit down to a table of
plenty without a thought to his own health, not realizing that
a modern loaf of white bread has had 95 percent of its vitamin B_6 processed out. Refined flour has lost 80 percent of its
original magnesium content. H. Borsook has shown that
many "poor" diets in the United States provide less than 1.0
milligram of vitamin B_6 daily, and some offer as little as 0.7
milligram daily.[2]

The relationship between the female hormone estrogen,
protein metabolism, and vitamin B_6 is extremely important.
When protein is not properly broken down, toxemia will
become evident in a number of different ways. This is especially true in pregnant women. During pregnancy, ductless
glands produce greater amounts of the various hormones.
Protein metabolism must be perfect for both the expectant
mother and her unborn infant to remain healthy. Daily mineral intake with attention to magnesium, one of the significant cofactors of B_6, and potassium is also important.[3]

Over fifty years ago, the most common problem associated
with pregnancy was already being studied in England and
treated with vitamins. In the July 22, 1944, edition of the

Journal of the American Medical Association, M.M. Marbel reported that when pregnant patients suffering from constant nausea were given injections of B_1 daily, their vomiting ceased after the fourth or fifth injection in every case. A much later study reported in the *American Journal of Obstetrics and Gynecology* noted that complete relief from nausea and vomiting was achieved by the administration of 25 to 100 milligrams of B_1 along with 50 milligrams of B_6. Two of the patients in this latter study were also relieved of accompanying migraine headaches, and none of the patients suffered any bad side effects.[4]

In a recent edition of the journal published by the American Academy of Family Physicians, an article out of the University of Alabama School of Medicine in Tuscaloosa noted forty-two listed causes of peripheral edema (abnormal retention of fluid in the feet, legs, hands, and arms). In three of the causes, the swelling was attributed to malnutrition, preeclampsia, and idiopathic (cause unknown) edema.[5] Preeclampsia, a disorder of pregnancy, is characterized by severe swelling of the hands and feet that may lead to deadly convulsions. A number of scientists have determined that vitamin B_6 regulates and, to a degree, controls the movement of hormones into tissues and thereby controls edema.

The most exciting day of my life was May 26, 1962, when I observed and treated a thirty-seven-year-old woman who was eight months pregnant and suffering from massive edema in her feet, legs, hands, and arms.[6] The woman complained of numbness and tingling from her hands to her elbows and stated that she had cramps in the muscles of her lower legs at night. The puffy swelling in her feet and hands was obvious. In order to be certain that this patient was getting vitamin B_6 into her bloodstream in the exact dosage I prescribed, I ordered an injection of 50 milligrams of the vitamin every other day. The woman had no other treatment. By June 12, all the edema in the feet and hands was gone, all the numbness and tingling had subsided, and the painful nighttime leg cramps had stopped.

A few days later, another woman, twenty-one years of age and eight months pregnant, came into my office complaining of edema in her hands and feet. Her right hand "would go to sleep while writing," she complained. And, she said, she frequently dropped dishes, breaking them. This dropping of objects during pregnancy is often reported to obstetricians. Again, to ensure delivery of an exact dosage into her bloodstream, I prescribed an injection of 50 milligrams of vitamin B$_6$ every other day. Following two weeks of treatment, the patient reported she could now hold onto plates, and the numbness, which she had described as being "like pins and needles" sticking into her arm, was gone. She said she still had a little numbness in the fingers of her right hand, but emphasized that she could now straighten her fingers after holding an umbrella, something she could not do before taking the shots. In addition, where before she had had to hang her arm over the side of the bed because of the pain, which had kept her awake, she could now comfortably lie with her arm at her side.

In other patients who received vitamin-B$_6$ injections, the objective evidence concerning their edema was connected to their wedding rings. A number of the patients had had to remove their rings because of the swelling in their fingers. Following treatment with vitamin-B$_6$ injections, they could replace their rings on their now-edema-free fingers. The same spectacular results were observed in patients who had taken 50 to 300 milligrams of vitamin B$_6$ by mouth every day.

The human body, when working properly, can handle as much as eight quarts of water a day without difficulty. Normally, six out of every ten pounds of body weight is water. But when the body's water-regulating system is altered or interfered with, the retained water seeks the places of least resistance in which to settle. The most common cause of generalized edema is premenstrual fluid retention. Both the physical and emotional symptoms of premenstrual fluid retention are related to the body's level of estrogen during the second half of the menstrual cycle. Estrogen is also a potent sodium-retaining hormone. The body's natural tendency when the sodium level rises is to dilute the sodium by retaining water.[7] Some scientists refer to this water balancing as the body's "sodium pump." It is possible that vitamin B_6 changes the sodium pump and naturally corrects the fluid exchange. Although water pills eliminate water buildup, they also overwork the kidneys and lead to a loss of important minerals. Therefore, it is better to use vitamin B_6, which blocks the estrogen-sodium cycle. A pregnant woman with edema should be given 300 milligrams of vitamin B_6 daily, along with 500 milligrams of magnesium oxide as an adjunctive supplement.[8]

On May 3, 1969, at the 102nd Annual Session of the Texas Medical Association in San Antonio, Texas, I read the following article synopsis to the Section on Obstetrics and Gynecology:

During pregnancy, pyridoxine (vitamin B_6) given 50 to 300 milligrams daily advantageously affected edema, muscle spasms, paresthesia of hands, painful finger joints, incoordination of hand movements, and abnormal weight gains. Pyridoxine caused regression of edema in five cases of toxemia of pregnancy, and convulsions ceased in a single case of eclampsia following intravenous administration of pyridoxine at six-hour intervals.

In 1984 in New Orleans and in 1985 in Orlando, I addressed, respectively, the 78th and 79th Annual Scientific Assembly of the Southern Medical Association. My reports were to the effect that over a period of nine years, I gave 50 to 200 milligrams of vitamin B_6 daily as a supplement to 225 pregnant women. The vitamin was found to improve the pregnancy-related edema in some of the women, as indicated by weight reductions of up to ten to fifteen pounds within two weeks of initiation of the treatment. In some way, the vitamin

assisted the excretion of edema fluid through the kidneys. My
final conclusion was that because it takes twelve weeks of vit-
amin-B$_6$ therapy to effect optimum clinical improvement of
carpal tunnel syndrome during and following pregnancy, 200
milligrams daily of vitamin B$_6$ should be prescribed as soon as
pregnancy is diagnosed in order to prevent pregnancy-related
edema and carpal tunnel syndrome. My report was published
in the *Southern Medical Journal* in 1987.

It should also be noted that during the course of the study
just mentioned, 25 of the pregnant women reported definite
improvements in their severe signs and symptoms of carpal
tunnel syndrome before giving birth.[9] A reduction in the
swelling in the hands and feet of pregnant women can be
observed within a week, sometimes in less than seventy-two
hours, of the initiation of vitamin-B$_6$ therapy. But swelling in
the synovium, the cause of carpal tunnel syndrome, is of a
different biochemical nature and does not subside as quickly.
In fact, for carpal tunnel syndrome, the dosage of B$_6$ is not as
important as its daily intake over a period of many weeks. It
is far better to prevent carpal tunnel syndrome at the beginning of pregnancy using a daily dose of 150 milligrams of vitamin B$_6$ than to treat it in the presence of toxemia during the
final days of pregnancy. And the diabetic pregnant patient is
in even greater need of B$_6$, as she is more prone to carpal tunnel syndrome and edema.

Laboratory tests have established that there is a close relationship between pregnancy and vitamin-B$_6$ deficiency.
When tryptophan is given to pregnant women, they experience an abnormal excretion of xanthurenic acid in the
urine.[10,11] In other words, a high percentage of pregnant
women are deficient in vitamin B$_6$. The female hormones are
very high during pregnancy and toxic in the presence of B$_6$
deficiency.

Women need more B$_6$ when their estrogen levels are increased, whether from pregnancy or the use of birth control
pills. Dr. P.W. Adams of St. Mary's Hospital Medical School in

London explained in 1975 at the Fourth International Congress on Hormonal Steroids that the hormone estrogen found in contraceptive pills increases the metabolism of tryptophan. This can result in a B_6 deficiency that is so severe it sometimes even upsets the delicate balance of the brain's chemistry, toppling the contraceptive user into depression. However, Dr. Adams' rigorous clinical studies showed that B_6 supplementation can restore mental equilibrium.[12] Every time a woman takes an anti-ovulatory pill, she should also take a B_6 tablet. The two might well be combined by the pharmaceutical houses into a single medication.

The RDA of vitamin B_6 for pregnant women set by the National Research Council is only 2.5 milligrams per day. The amount of B_6 needed to meet the requirements of a fetus is unknown. According to a study done by Dr. Robert E. Cleary and his associates, as reported in the January 1975 issue of the *American Journal of Obstetrics and Gynecology*, babies delivered by women who took a 10.0-milligram supplement of vitamin B_6 daily were proven to have 50-percent-higher levels of B_6 in their umbilical cords than did the babies delivered by women who took just the RDA. J.A. Kleiger and his associates found that the placentas from women who had toxemia of pregnancy contained less vitamin B_6 than did the placentas from women who did not have toxemia.[13] More recently, A. Kirksey and S.A. Udipi reported that pregnant women require 4.0 milligrams of vitamin B_6 per day, and that some require up to 10.0 milligrams per day, to normalize both fetal and maternal metabolic needs.[14] It is also known that preterm infants have extremely low levels of B_6 at birth, and that B_6 deficiencies in newborns may cause spasms that often can be alleviated by daily administration of 50 to 100 milligrams of B_6.[15] And it must be emphasized that expectant mothers should not consume alcohol. Alcohol prevents the interaction of phosphorus and vitamin B_6 in the mother, and damages the brain of the unborn child. Vitamin B_6 is very important in the brain development of infants, both before and after birth.

Following the Vietnam War, a returning young combat veteran came to work as a ranch foreman near Mt. Pleasant. Under the care of other physicians, his wife suffered five spontaneous and early miscarriages in succession. For reasons unknown, the couple had no children after five years of marriage. With the understanding that many pregnant women had been proven deficient in vitamin B$_6$, I prescribed 600 milligrams of B$_6$ daily in divided doses for twelve days, to be followed by 300 milligrams daily. Two months later, the young woman became pregnant.

In 1973, at term pregnancy, the cowboy's wife delivered a normal female infant without complications. She continued to take vitamin B$_6$ postpartum at a dose of 300 milligrams daily. Then, in 1977, she again gave birth without complications, this time to a normal male infant. There was no edema of pregnancy. This followed four years of treatment with 300 milligrams of vitamin B$_6$ daily. In the spring of 1998, both the daughter and son were college honor students, the daughter at Northeast Texas Community College School of Nursing in Titus County on a full scholarship paid for by the Titus Regional Medical Center.

Quite recently, physicians and scientists at a university hospital began a study of the elevation of homocysteine in one hundred consecutive miscarriage patients. It was found that 20 percent of the women studied had a gene defect of an enzyme that is normally dependent on folic acid. Treatment with folic acid and vitamin B$_6$ normalized the homocysteine concentration and favored successful pregnancy. A scientific article published in January 1988 concluded that elevated homocysteine should be identified in women with recurrent miscarriages because therapeutic normalization might permit a normal birth.[16]

Many weeks are required for B$_6$ to begin helping the body to fully utilize the enzymes present during pregnancy. Of vital importance is the fact that the protein in the blood serum of a newborn infant must come from the blood of the mother. The total protein in the blood serum of a new mother ranges from 6.0 to 8.0 grams percent. The total protein in the blood serum of a normal newborn is 4.6 to 7.4 grams percent. "Grams percent" is a laboratory figure used in the determination of the amount of protein in blood serum. A low figure indicates the need for more blood protein. At birth, an infant must have enzymes ready to receive and metabolize the protein in breast milk or formula.[17]

Vitamin B_6 is so important during pregnancy that, in my opinion—to prevent carpal tunnel syndrome and edema, and to ensure the biochemical relationships necessary to balance out the increase in the steroid hormones—all expectant mothers should take 200 milligrams of vitamin B_6 daily. If the mother-to-be has gestational diabetes or diabetes mellitus, she should take 300 milligrams of B_6 daily. Pregnant women have a marked increase in the female hormones and need sufficient amounts of vitamin B_6 to counterbalance them. In diabetic pregnant women, this is even more important, since the steroid hormones can contribute to blindness if vitamin B_6 is deficient. There are many complications associated with the combination of pregnancy and diabetes, which makes a strong case for routine supplementation with B_6 by all women of child-bearing age.

Reporting to the Third World Congress of Perinatal Medicine in 1996, Dr. Ute Schaefer of the University of Southern California School of Medicine stated that the degree of hyperglycemia at the time gestational diabetes is diagnosed directly correlates with the risk of major congenital anomalies (birth defects). It was known at the time that glycemic control during pregnancy in women with insulin-dependent or non-insulin-dependent diabetes correlates with the risk of fetal malformations. However, the relationship had not yet been established for gestational diabetes. Dr. Schaefer said that women with fasting serum-glucose levels of 120 to 260 milligrams per deciliter at the time of diagnosis of gestational diabetes have more than twice the risk of having an infant with a major congenital anomaly than do women with lower glucose levels. She and her associates looked at the glycemic variables in 4,229 women with gestational diabetes. Infants with anomalies caused by chromosomal abnormalities such as genetic syndromes and aneuploidies were excluded from the analysis. Of the remaining 288 infants born with anomalies, 117 had major anomalies that caused significant morbidity (disease) and/or required surgical correction.[18]

These are horrible figures on birth defects. The chemistries involve the steroid hormones estrogen, progesterone, and cortisone. Without question, there is a relationship between vitamin B_6 and these hormones. The relationship is as follows: The human body normally makes the female steroid hormones estrogen, progesterone, corticosterone, and cortisol in the ovaries and adrenal glands. These hormones enter into the DNA of the cells of many tissues. This affects gene expression (the job a gene does inside the body). Vitamin B_6 even in trace amounts can regulate, block, or even remove some amounts of these hormones when they are produced in normal quantities. However, during pregnancy, these hormones are produced in increased amounts and trace amounts of vitamin B_6 are no longer effective.[19–24]

Regarding the female hormones and edema in relation to menstruation, 50 to 200 milligrams of vitamin B_6 taken daily prevents premenstrual edema. This was proven by nurses who took vitamin B_6 at Titus County Memorial Hospital in Mt. Pleasant, Texas. Here, again, a marvelous and natural biochemical relationship between the female hormones and vitamin B_6 was established at the time of menopause. When the ovaries cease to function, a common complaint is "hot flushes," caused by the reduction in hormones including estrogen. Menstruation becomes irregular and then stops. After menstruation ceases due to menopause, there is a gradual reduction in six steroid hormones and five pituitary hormones over a period of twenty to eighty months. In other words, there is gradual reduction in hormone levels over the six years following menopause.[25]

Clinicians have been searching for all kinds of disease conditions that improve with estrogen and other hormone therapy. But the flag horse in the parade of signs and symptoms is menopausal arthritis, which affects the hands and fingers. The stiffness, noted in and around the finger joints, is caused by changes in the connective tissue around the joints. Dense fibrous tissue replaces the youthful elastic tissues. There is some swelling and edema, and pain upon flexing the joints. When treated with 100 to 200 milligrams of vitamin B_6 daily, this menopausal arthritis is relieved. The finger joints are no longer painful, and flexion is improved. In effect, vitamin B_6 works in conjunction with the remaining female hormones to preserve the elastic tissues, not only in the hands, but in other parts of the body including the arteries. Elastic fibrils are necessary in the walls of the arteries, both large and small, to keep the arteries responsive to the pulsation of the blood in the heart and brain in both women and men.

The most elastic tissue responsive to hormones in the human is the cervix at the lower end of the uterus. Before pregnancy, a gynecologist cannot put his or her finger through this opening into the uterus, but at the time of delivery, a baby's head can slip through. The wide opening of the cervix is the youthful and elastic response to the female hormones secreted during pregnancy. For this response, however, vitamin B_6 must also be present in sufficient quantity to work in conjunction with the hormones.

Going back to the subject of animal husbandry, it is interesting to note that there is more estrogen in the testicle of a stallion than in any other known tissue. This hormone helps to preserve the elastic fibrils in the horse from his head to his tail. There is even a puzzling little fact of endocrinology that may indicate that men, too, routinely require more B_6 for health than is currently believed. This fact is that there is one-half as much estradiol, a female hormone, in the urine of men as there is in the urine of women. It is known that estrogen given to men with cancer of the prostate gland is helpful in the control of the cancer. However, the testicles are surgically removed in some men with this cancer. After the age of fifty, almost everyone needs more vitamin B$_6$. In the 1960s, Dr. Ronald Searcy, director of diagnostic research at Hoffmann–La Roche, Inc., pointed out that blood-plasma levels of B$_6$ average 11.3 millimicrograms per milliliter in persons between the ages of twenty and twenty-nine. But after age thirty, the levels drop to 7.1, and by age sixty, they drop to 3.4.

At the Institute for Biomedical Research at the University of Texas in Austin, it has been proven that it takes six to eight weeks of vitamin-B$_6$ therapy to get the important enzyme EGOT up to maximum activity. Vitamin B$_6$ assists enzymes in moving lysine to the molecules of collagen and elastin in connective tissue, the cartilage in joints, the synovium around tendons, and the matrix between cells.[26] Human organs such as the ovaries, the adrenal glands, the pancreas, and the pituitary gland all depend on thirty enzymatic reactions for the proper production of hormones—and *all* of them depend on vitamin B$_6$. Vitamin B$_6$, the protein vitamin, may well be the miracle vitamin of the next century. It is a magnificent maestro amid a symphony of endocrine glands, each playing its tone or undertone in life's most marvelous arrangement.[27]

Chapter 6

DIABETES

According to the American Diabetes Association, the 1998 statistics show that an estimated 16 million Americans suffer from diabetes, and half of them don't even know it. Between 1990 and 1992, approximately 625,000 new cases of diabetes were diagnosed annually, with an equal number left undiagnosed. Diabetes mellitus is increasing and spreading throughout the United States. In comparison with the general population, diabetics are two to four times more likely to suffer a heart attack, two to three times more likely to have a stroke, and two times more likely to need a leg amputation. Diabetes is the leading cause of blindness and end-stage kidney disease in the United States. This high incidence of complications explains in part why 15 percent of the entire healthcare budget is devoted to diabetes.[1]

Studies on vitamin B_6 provide insights into the diabetic dilemma. Clinical tests have proven that vitamin-B_6 deficiency is common in both type I and type II diabetes, each of which is related to sugar metabolism. In type I (insulin-dependent or juvenile) diabetes, the pancreas does not produce enough insulin, and in the later stages, it does not produce insulin at all. In type II (non-insulin-dependent) diabetes, the pancreas does produce insulin, but the insulin is ineffective. Both type I and type II diabetes require tight dietary control of carbohydrate consumption, as documented by the Diabetes Control and Complications Trial (DCCT) Research Group.[2]

However, tight control is not enough. The best figure that the DCCT Research Group could secure was that the use of tight control methods slowed the development of diabetic retinopathy in 54 percent of the patients tested, which means that 46 percent went on to develop advanced diabetic retinopathy. This is important because the presence of diabetic retinopathy indicates that the diabetes has progressed beyond mere sugar control. Also important to note is that 85 percent of newly diagnosed diabetics are age forty-five or older,[3] while the diabetics in the DCCT study were twenty-seven years old, plus or minus seven years.[4] The fact that tight dietary control and intensive insulin therapy were not successful in halting diabetic retinopathy in a high percentage of the cases studied prompted an evaluation of research I had conducted on the use of vitamin B$_6$ in the prevention and treatment of diabetic retinopathy.

In my study, which began in 1989, several colleagues and I tested twenty-one patients with diabetes mellitus, either type I or type II, for vitamin-B$_6$ deficiency and treated them accordingly. I was with these patients so often and for so long that I came to think and speak of them as the "Magnificent Twenty-One."

From November 1989 to November 1991, I worked in collaboration with ophthalmologist Michael Minadeo, internist Ronald Van Buskirk, and biochemist Karl Folkers to complete an intensive in-depth study of the whole bodies of these twenty-one patients. The age at onset of diabetes for these patients ranged from five years to seventy-three years. One patient had taken vitamin B$_6$ daily for twenty-eight years, while another had taken it for only a few days. All the patients except one either continued or began taking 100 to 300 milligrams of vitamin B_6 daily as part of the study. The subject who refused to take B_6 became, in effect, the negative control in the study. She had the lowest EGOT level (0.15) of any patient in the study. The enzyme EGOT is necessary for vitamin-B_6 metabolism and, through a correlation of the signs and symptoms of diabetes with the precise activity of the enzyme, can assist in the determination of vitamin-B_6 deficiency.[5-9]

All the patients in the study had blood samples taken and sent to Dr. Folkers at the University of Texas for EGOT testing.[10] Different kinds of blood and urine chemistries were recorded, and the retinas of the eyes were studied by ophthalmologists in Mt. Pleasant and at the University of Texas Southwestern Medical School in Dallas. Each patient also underwent fluorescein angiogram studies of the tiny blood vessels in the retinas of the eyes. (For a diagram of the eye, see Figure 6.1.) In a fluorescein angiogram study, a dye is injected into the vein of the arm and pictures of the retinas are made a few seconds later.

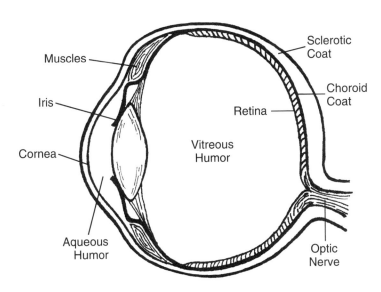

Figure 6.1. The anatomy of the eye.

The ending test results were nothing short of fantastic. Over the two-year study period, repeated fluorescein angiogram studies showed that there was virtually no leakage of dye into or around the macula lutea. The macula lutea is located near the center of the retina and is the point at which visual perception is the most acute. (See Figure 6.2.) It is the precise point of central vision. Central vision is used, for example, by a hawk at sunrise peering at a field mouse far below or a child keeping track of a distant firefly at dusk. Macular edema is the leading cause of impaired central vision in the United States and leads to diabetic blindness.[11] Therefore, the macula lutea is an important place for macular edema to be controlled.

Critics would ask for a control study and conclusive evidence that vitamin B$_6$ kept the tiny arteries in the retina from leaking fluid, fatty substances, and cholesterol into and around the macula lutea. The positive answer is that the vision of the twenty-one subjects was frequently tested by ophthalmologists and their assistants. The visual acuities were found to be virtually unchanged, if not improved, during the two years the patients received therapeutic doses of vitamin B$_6$, even though some of the subjects had high blood-

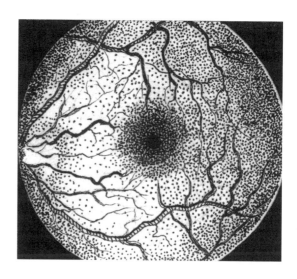

Figure 6.2. This diagram of a left retina shows arteries and veins adjacent to the white optic nerve on the left. The round, cupped, darkened area in the center is the macula lutea.

sugar levels. And remember, there was a control study—BS, the patient who refused to take vitamin B_6. Diagnosed at five years of age, BS was found to have type I diabetes.

At age twenty, BS had become pregnant and suffered severe pregnancy-related edema. She was pregnant twice and delivered both babies by cesarean section. Both infants died. At age twenty-nine, BS had taken estrogen, as prescribed by a physician. At age thirty, she had had laser surgery performed on the retinas in the backs of both eyes. Two years later, she developed carpal tunnel syndrome in both hands. She took vitamin B_6 for only a few days, then stopped and never took a vitamin or mineral supplement again. At the time of that decision, she was a clerk-typist and had to quit typing. In 1988, BS had surgery on both hands at the carpal tunnels that brought relief from the pain, paresthesia, numbness, and tingling, but was followed by severe stiffness. (See Figure 6.3.) In December 1989, when she was admitted to our clinical study, the flexion of her index fingers at the proximal

Figure 6.3.
In this photograph taken in December 1989, patient BS cannot fully extend her fingers because of stiffness.

joints was measured by goniometer and found to be 0 to 86 degrees in both the right and left hands. (See Figure 6.4.) The normal range is 0 to 105 degrees. Her pinch, measured with a Preston Pinch Gauge, was found to be 4.8 pounds in the left hand and 3.5 pounds in the right hand. The normal pinch is 8 to 10 pounds. BS had loss of flexion and severe crippling in her hands even after the bilateral carpal-tunnel surgery, and her vision was steadily deteriorating despite the laser surgery. (See Figure 6.5.)

Again, with emphasis, BS took no vitamin B_6. She had the lowest initial EGOT blood level of any patient in the study, laboratory proof that this negative-control patient had severe vitamin-B_6 deficiency. She suffered acute myocardial infarction with cardiac arrest and underwent a heart transplant in July 1990. After the transplant, she was given huge doses of hydrocortisone and synthetic prednisone to help prevent rejection of the transplanted heart. In 1992, she took 0.625 milligram of estrogen and 7.0 milligrams of prednisone daily. In 1993, proliferation and abnormal new growth of tiny arteries led to hemorrhage in the right retina. In addition, the deterioration in vision finally ended in diabetic blindness. On

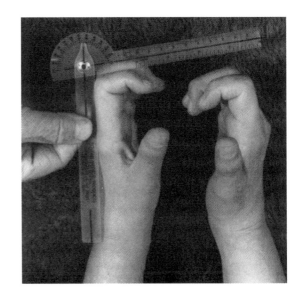

Figure 6.4. In December 1989, BS also could flex her fingers only from 0 to 86 degrees, as measured by goniometer, instead of the normal 0 to 105 degrees.

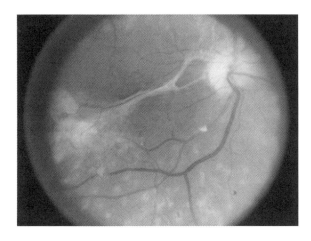

Figure 6.5.
This December
1989 photograph
of BS's right
retina shows a
dense fibrotic
preretinal
membrane
extending from
the optic nerve
through the fovea
centralis of the
macula lutea.

August 22, 1993, after thirty-years (since age five) of having diabetes mellitus type I, BS died of severe coronary artery disease. The final diagnosis was that her death was due to coronary heart disease caused by calcification and blockage in the coronary arteries, diabetes mellitus type I, and severe vitamin-B_6 deficiency. The last two conditions had crippled, blinded, and killed members of three generations of her family.

The case histories of all the "Magnificent Twenty-One" could fill a whole volume by themselves. Therefore, I will limit my further discussion of the study subjects to specific points of interest and diagnosis.

One interesting subject was TS. TS was married at fifteen years of age, experienced an intolerance to birth control pills, and became pregnant at age eighteen. While pregnant, she developed severe pregnancy-related edema and was diagnosed with type I diabetes. She took insulin for fifteen years and had diabetic retinopathy when she entered our study in 1989. Her EGOT test proved that she had a serious vitamin-B_6 deficiency. She also had severe carpal tunnel syndrome in both hands. (See Figure 6.6.) Numbness kept her from being able to turn off her alarm clock in the morning.

At the beginning of the study, TS took 100 milligrams of vitamin-B_6 daily. By the end of the study, in 1992, she took 200 milligrams daily. Within ninety days of beginning the treat-

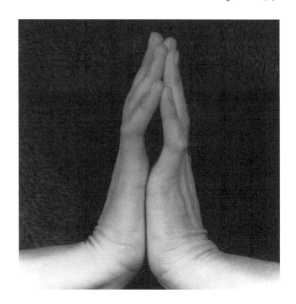

Figure 6.6.
This 1989 photograph shows that patient TS had limited finger-joint extension when she first entered the "Magnificent Twenty-One" study.

ment, she found all the signs and symptoms of carpal tunnel syndrome resolved. (See Figure 6.7.) Her finger function had improved. When we initially reviewed TS's case, we learned that she had begun losing protein through her kidneys in 1986. At the time she entered the study, her twenty-four-hour urine protein loss was very serious, and it remained serious even though she took 200 milligrams of vitamin B_6 daily. TS also had more eye surgeries than any other patient in the study. However, when the study was over, TS continued to take 200 milligrams of B_6 daily and, as late as 1997, eight years after beginning the B_6 therapy, her vision was excellent, with no sign of macular edema. She experienced no recurrence of the carpal tunnel syndrome, and her formerly weak fingernails were amazingly long. Tragic, however, was TS's continuing loss of protein through the kidneys and her need for dialysis while waiting for a kidney transplant.

Of the "Magnificent Twenty-One," seven patients had classic carpal tunnel syndrome. Six of the seven (excluding BS, the negative-control patient) were given therapeutic doses of vitamin B_6. Six of the seven were women. All six of the patients with carpal tunnel syndrome who took the thera-

Figure 6.7.
This photograph shows that TS recovered the ability to fully extend her fingers after taking 100 milligrams of vitamin B_6 daily for just thirty-two days.

peutic vitamin-B_6 treatment were cured of their carpal tunnel syndrome. In addition, their loss of flexibility associated with diabetes was also cured.

RS, another study patient, was married to TS. RS also suffered from type I diabetes, diagnosed when he was seventeen years old. Before entering the study, he had been hospitalized ten different times because his blood sugar was dangerously high. By November 1989, when he joined the study, he was twenty-six years old, had been taking insulin for nine years, and had minimal diabetic retinopathy. His wife described him as "very depressed," so depressed, in fact, that he had not been able to work for two years.

The laboratory data were extremely important in RS's case. In 1986, another physician had prescribed a multi-vitamin-and-mineral supplement that included 3.0 milligrams of vitamin B_6 per tablet. Assuming that RS got 1.5 milligrams of B_6 from his food per day, he probably consumed a total of 4.5 milligrams of B_6 daily. The initial blood sample taken in 1989 showed that RS's EGOT blood level was exactly what one would expect with this amount of B_6 intake. RS was advised to take 100 milligrams of B$_6$ daily beginning December 4, 1989.

Within a few weeks of beginning the increased dosage, RS began to feel more strength and energy. In addition, his mental depression seemed to lift. During 1990, RS performed hard labor even in hot weather, missing only ten days work, and these due to mild respiratory infections. In 1991, his vitamin-B$_6$ dosage was increased to 200 milligrams daily. On October 11, 1991, RS had perfect twenty-twenty vision in both eyes and no evidence of macular edema. His EGOT test showed a vitamin-B$_6$ blood level that had almost doubled since his first test. But something terrible was happening to his kidneys. Urine chemistries done in January 1992 showed that he was excreting large amounts of protein. Nine months later, RS had a blinding hemorrhage in his right eye that could not be corrected. Dialysis was begun on a daily basis in November 1994, and five laser surgeries were performed on the left eye over a period of two months. Then, on October 1, 1995, RS had a successful kidney transplant. "I feel better than I have in years," RS reported. He was still blind in his right eye because of the hemorrhage, but the vision in his left eye was twenty-twenty.

At this point in our discussion, serious evaluation is due and several questions need to be answered. Were there any type I diabetics in the study who responded better to the vitamin-B$_6$ therapy as far as prevention is concerned? Can diabetes be prevented with vitamin B$_6$? What would happen if therapeutic dosages of vitamin B$_6$ were given before diabetes became apparent or was diagnosed?

I will use patient DE to answer these questions. At the age of fourteen, to relieve leg cramps, DE had begun taking 100 milligrams of vitamin B$_6$ daily. He had continued this practice even after his leg cramps had resolved. At the age of twenty, DE developed type I diabetes. His mother had been diagnosed with type II diabetes at the age of fifty-two. In 1990, DE was placed on 300 milligrams of vitamin B$_6$ daily.

Note that at the time of diagnosis, he had been taking vitamin B$_6$ for six years already, and continued to take it at the onset of diabetes. He never had diabetic retinopathy or macular edema. He never needed laser surgery. His vision remained perfect through August 1997, which was twenty years after his original diagnosis. Also important is that all of his blood and urine chemistries, completed at the University of Texas Southwestern Medical School, were normal, except for an occasional elevated blood-sugar level, which still was never in the danger zone. In summary, DE took 100 to 300 milligrams of vitamin B$_6$ daily for twenty-six years, enduring diabetes mellitus type I for twenty years and reaching the age of forty without kidney damage or the severe complications of crippling or blindness.

I should mention that among the "Magnificent Twenty-One" were two patients with type II diabetes who took therapeutic dosages of vitamin B$_6$ for several years prior to the onset of their diabetes. The major conclusion we can reach, therefore, is that vitamin B$_6$ can prevent the severe complications of diabetes if it is taken early enough, but it cannot prevent the onset of diabetes.

As examples of the use of vitamin B$_6$ in the prevention and treatment of the severe complications of type II diabetes, two patients, MS and CE, are outstanding. MS was found to have type II diabetes at the age of fifty-one. Eight years later, she had a near-fatal automobile accident in which she suffered an irreparable detached right optic nerve resulting in blindness. MS took 60 units of insulin and 100 milligrams of vitamin B$_6$ daily. By March 1, 1991, she had been taking vitamin B$_6$ for seventeen years, with her dosage recently increased to 300 milligrams daily. Her EGOT test showed maximum compliance on her part. The near vision in her left eye was a perfect twenty–twenty-five, and there was no macular edema. On November 18, 1994, MS was eighty years old, had had type II diabetes for twenty-nine years, and had been taking 100 to 300 milligrams of vitamin B$_6$ daily for twenty years. With glasses, her left eye was tested at a splendid twenty-forty for distant vision and twenty-thirty for near vision. With pleasure, she could read the newspaper. She had never required ophthalmic surgery. Fluorescein angiogram studies done at age eighty showed slight leakage in the periphery of the left retina, but no pooling of fluorescein in the macula lutea. The fovea centralis, composed of the smallest, most visually selective, and extremely sensitive nerve cells in the eye, was clear. This meant MS had no macular edema.

CE, the other type II diabetic, came to be one of the most monumental patients in the "Magnificent Twenty-One" study. CE was a great-grandson of my Grandfather Ellis's lifelong friend Sam Ellis. My grandfather and Sam had raised hogs and sheep in the White Oak and Sulphur River bottoms for many years. Sam's great-grandson had worked hard labor in the cotton fields. This family, as I related in Chapter 1, had a history of long life, which I attributed to a diet that included wheat hulls, high in vitamin B_6. But CE was a man of his time, and hog shorts had long since disappeared from his table. In 1980, at the age of sixty-two, CE was diagnosed with diabetes.

In January 1989, CE was taking 50 milligrams of vitamin B_6 daily, as well as 30 units of insulin in the morning and 15 units in the evening. He continually put off seeking medical attention and developed gangrene in both of his feet. On January 4, 1990, his EGOT test showed a maximum enzyme level for vitamin B_6—proof that he had been taking his B_6. His vision was twenty–two hundred in the right eye and twenty–one hundred in the left eye. He had cataracts in both eyes and advanced diabetic retinopathy in both eyes preproliferative—that is, he had an overgrowth of tiny arteries in the back of the eyes. In addition, he had focal leakage of fluid in the macular area, more in the left eye than in the right eye.

A general surgeon amputated CE's left leg below the knee and put a skin graft on the right foot. On January 30, 1990, a retinal specialist performed photocoagulation (surgical coagulation of tissue using a laser beam) on the left retina.

Because laser surgery was performed on the left eye but not on the right, we were able to compare, to a certain degree, the two eyes of a patient who had been taking 50 milligrams of vitamin B$_6$ daily for a year. On January 12, 1991, an EGOT test again indicated that CE had been faithful in taking his B$_6$. There was no overgrowth of tiny arteries in the right eye. However, a second laser operation was done on the retina of the left eye. In March and April 1991, the cataracts were removed from both eyes. On May 6, 1991, the opthalmologist, Dr. Minadeo, reported that CE's "right retina appears better than when the patient went to Dallas 16 months previously."

At this point, CE had been taking 50 milligrams of vitamin B$_6$ daily for twenty-nine months. The retinal specialist and Dr. Minadeo agreed that much of the loss of vision in CE's eyes had been due to the cataracts. Only after their removal could an accurate determination be made of the vitreous and of the retina behind the vitreous. (See Figure 6.1 on page 71.) Removing cataracts does not always improve vision in diabetic patients. In fact, vision sometimes becomes worse following cataract extraction when the patient has diabetic retinopathy. Hypertension often adds to the complications of diabetic retinopathy, and systemic inflammation can increase diabetic retinopathy including macular edema.

CE had all of these complications. Proof of discovery with vitamin B$_6$ would be difficult because of the different complications involved, including changes in the inflammation and gangrene in the foot. In other words, several conditions were going on, and evaluation of each condition was difficult in relationship to the treatment with vitamin B$_6$ over a period of years. Furthermore, a number of the changes taking place were due to aging. CE's insulin requirement had increased, and he was now taking 35 units in the morning and 20 units in the evening. An encouraging note was that the inflammation in his right foot and leg had subsided and the skin graft on his right foot was in excellent condition. Realizing that a showdown was near, I had to obtain the opinions of two ophthalmologists. I also had to determine if raising CE's vitamin-B_6 dosage would in any way improve the condition of his eyes. On June 7, 1991, I increased the B_6 dosage to 300 milligrams daily.

On July 31, 1991, Dr. Minadeo conducted a crucial ophthalmic examination of CE. He noted that CE's right eye had dried out. The macular edema had subsided. The buildup of exudate (crust) caused by the leakage of fluid, fatty streaks, and cholesterol deposits from the tiny arteries on the temporal side of the retina had disappeared. And this was without laser surgery.

I was thrilled. Macular edema in both eyes had been described by both ophthalmologists in January 1990. But Dr. Minadeo, sitting on a stool before CE, now turned to me and said, "You can hang your hat on this case. The vision has been stabilized and maintained throughout the treatments and observations." CE's distant vision in the right eye with glasses was a spectacular twenty-thirty. CE by this time had been taking 300 milligrams of vitamin B_6 daily for fifty-four days.

By October 10, 1991, CE had been taking 300 milligrams of vitamin B_6 daily for four months. Dr. Minadeo again examined his eyes. With exuberance bordering on excitement, the doctor called for the last set of photographs taken before CE's cataracts had been extracted. He studied the photographs and then examined the patient's eyes again. "At the present time, the maculas are dry," Dr. Minadeo announced. "The retinal vascular status has improved markedly since May. Pannetinal photocoagulation in the left eye reduced blot and dot hemorrhages. There is no proliferative retinopathy in either eye."

In all truth, CE had received splendid care during the nineteen months since entering the study. The proof was the fact that he could walk, read a newspaper, and watch television with pleasure. On October 22, 1991, at the James Aston Ambulatory Care Center at the University of Texas Medical Center in Dallas, a fluorescein angiogram study showed no macular edema in the fovea centralis of either macula lutea.

The case of CE provided clear evidence that a dosage of 300 milligrams of vitamin B$_6$ daily was more effective in controlling macular edema and retinopathy than 50 milligrams daily. CE had begun taking 50 milligrams of vitamin B$_6$ daily in 1989, and some degree of retinopathy had persisted. On October 10, 1991, after taking a daily supplement of 300 milligrams of vitamin B$_6$ for four months, since June 7, 1991, the diabetic retinopathy was markedly improved.

A follow-up examination conducted two years later was highly significant. During the two-year interval, CE had continued taking his 200 to 300 milligrams of vitamin B$_6$ daily. A comparison of the fluorescein angiogram studies made at this exam with those made earlier showed there was a spectacular reduction in the leakage of fluorescein in the right retina, which at no time had received photocoagulation. (See Figure 6.8.)

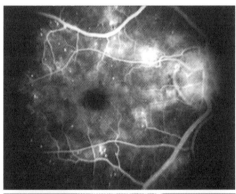

Figure 6.8.

Top photo:
This fluorescein angiogram taken of patient CE's right eye on July 29, 1991, shows extensive leakage of dye in the retina.

Bottom photo:
This follow-up fluorescein angiogram taken on August 19, 1993, after CE had been supplementing his diet with 200 to 300 milligrams of vitamin B$_6$ daily, shows virtually no leakage of dye in the right retina.

On February 22, 1995, five years after his leg amputation, CE could drive his automobile about town, watch his favorite television shows, and read the *Mt. Pleasant Daily Tribune*. There was no sign of infection around the skin graft. The diabetes was under control, with CE taking 30 units of insulin in the morning and 15 units in the evening. CE's distant vision without glasses was twenty-thirty in the right eye and twenty-forty in the left eye. With glasses, his near vision was twenty-thirty. These results indicated the continued prevention of macular edema in a seventy-seven-year-old man who for fifteen years had had diabetes mellitus type II.

Also impressive was the follow-up examination of MD, formerly a licensed vocational nurse. On July 22, 1997, MD was eighty years of age, had been taking a therapeutic dosage of vitamin B$_6$ for thirty-one years, and had had type II diabetes for seven years. A careful examination performed by an ophthalmologist at the Minadeo Eye Center in Mt. Pleasant showed that she had no evidence of diabetic retinopathy. Her vision without glasses was an excellent twenty–twenty-five in the right eye and twenty-thirty in the left eye. Laser surgery on the retinas had never been necessary. For almost a third of a century, this ex-nurse had taken 100 milligrams of vitamin B$_6$ daily as a supplement.

In summary, we can conclude from this study of the "Magnificent Twenty-One" that every diabetic at every stage should be given a therapeutic dosage of 100 to 300 milligrams of B$_6$ daily. A quick response to vitamin B$_6$ is not so evident in the late stages of diabetic retinopathy or nephropathy (kidney disease). However, it is in the prevention of these catastrophic conditions that vitamin B$_6$ becomes important. The rheumatic improvements seen within three months of beginning treatment with vitamin B$_6$ signal the long-term prevention of diabetic retinopathy and nephropathy.

The biochemistries and cellular activities in the different bodily tissues, including those of the eye, are responsive to a number of enzymatic activities. These enzymatic activities, many of which require vitamin B_6, affect the collagen in the vitreous and retina, and the matrix in the retina. This explains why one result of a long-term vitamin-B_6 deficiency is the leakage of serum and lipids including cholesterol into the vitreous and retina.

Teenagers do not experience extensive changes in the vitreous and retina, even when they are severely hyperglycemic, except in the presence of pregnancy or increased steroid-hormone activity. Vitamin B_6 must be present in therapeutic amounts for the regulation and modulation of the entry of steroid hormones into the vitreous and the retina in diabetic patients.[12]

Studies I had conducted earlier in which crippled hands responded to vitamin B_6 led me to the conclusion that B_6 regulates and modulates the movement of steroid hormones into the tissues.[13–15] Involved in this fabulous biochemistry is the protection of the cartilage in joints, the collagen and elastin in connective tissues, and the matrix that holds the cells together.

George Phalen, M.D., was the first to report that diabetes commonly accompanies carpal tunnel syndrome. He also reported that the majority of patients with carpal tunnel syndrome are women at or near menopause, and that the symptoms are aggravated by pregnancy. Hormonal changes seemed to play a causative role.[16]

Diabetic patients receiving vitamin-B_6 treatment have been cured of carpal tunnel syndrome. In addition, they have been cured of the loss of flexibility associated with diabetes. And evidence is now significant that patients who have taken 100 to 300 milligrams of vitamin B_6 daily for a period of years are more likely to survive acute myocardial infarction and live years longer than patients who have not followed this protocol.[17]

Diabetes affects the young and the old, male and female. Geneticists have not been able to prove that diabetes is a hereditary disease, although they have shown conclusively that minority populations are at higher risk. "Americans are incorrectly told their diabetes is due to genetic factors, yet diabetes is nearly nonexistent in human populations where the diet is centered around fiber-rich plant foods," writes Bill Sardi in an article arguing that there are other treatments for diabetes beyond insulin therapy and laser treatment, the two methods acknowledged by the American Diabetes Association to benefit diabetic retinopathy.[18] Other treatments *are* available, and vitamin B$_6$ is prominent among them.

The National Institute of Diabetes and Digestive and Kidney Diseases has concluded that the rise in minority populations, the prevalence of obesity, the aging of the population, and the decline in exercise are all factors that help explain why the number of cases of diabetes in the United States have more than tripled in the last thirty-five years.[19] It is now accepted by the scientific community that in the various stages of life and human development, vitamin-B$_6$ deficiency contributes to the origin and continuation of the complications of diabetes.

Chapter 7

CORONARY HEART DISEASE

It was about two o'clock in the afternoon on July 13, 1989, a hot summer day in eastern Texas. I was making a deposit at the Guaranty Bank in Mt. Pleasant. Suddenly, fifteen feet to my side, a young man crumpled to the floor. I first thought he was having some kind of seizure. I went to him, laid him on his back, and felt for his pulse. It was non-existent. He was not breathing, and his ears were turning blue. The young man was dying.

I knelt to the right of the young man and pinched his nose shut with my left thumb and forefinger to prevent any air from passing through. With my right hand, I pushed his chin down to open his mouth. I took a deep breath and blew into his lungs. My breath, although exhaled, still contained a certain amount of oxygen.

Another bank customer knelt down opposite me and placed her hands on the left side of the unconscious man's chest. With her arms straight and using the power of her weight, she rapidly pressed down on the man's chest four times, forcing some type of circulation into his heart. I didn't know it at the time, and was not surprised to find out later, that the young woman was a registered nurse who at one time had worked in the intensive care unit of a Dallas hospital.

The ex-nurse again vigorously pressed down on the man's chest four quick times. I drew in another deep breath and blew forcefully into his lungs. I yelled for someone to call an ambulance and then returned to performing what is known as cardiopulmonary resuscitation (CPR). It seemed like forever, but in reality it was only fifteen minutes later that two paramedics rushed through the bank door with emergency equipment. One of the paramedics immediately inserted a pliable tube into the man's trachea (windpipe) for immediate ventilation with oxygen. The other paramedic hooked the patient up to a cardiac monitor, which showed the man was experiencing ventricular fibrillation (the quivering of the heart muscle just before death). An electric shock administered by the paramedics jolted the man's heart muscle back into a normal rhythm.

The young man turned out to be only thirty-four years of age—three decades plus four—too young for the death that surely would have claimed him that afternoon had not someone been there to immediately begin CPR. While in the intensive care unit of the hospital, he was found to have a severe, 99-percent blockage in the main coronary artery on the left side of his heart. His heart muscle was not functioning well. Subsequently, he had open heart surgery to improve his coronary artery circulation.

Following his heart surgery, the young man seemed to improve, but the improvement was only temporary. A little more than five years later, he was anxiously awaiting a heart transplant when, while talking to a friend, he once more fell to the ground unconscious. This time, however, he wasn't so lucky. He was pronounced dead in the emergency room of Titus County Memorial Hospital. The cause of death was listed as a pulmonary embolism (a massive blood clot in the artery going from the heart to the lungs). The man was forty years old when he died.

For the record, all the physicians who attend patients in the intensive care unit of Titus County Memorial Hospital are certified in accordance with the American Heart Association Standards for Basic and Advanced Life Support. All the internists are additionally qualified as instructors for the American Heart Association Cardiopulmonary Resuscitation and Emergency Cardiac Care Program. By protocol, the patients admitted to the intensive care unit with cardiac chest pain or suspected acute myocardial infarction are given chest X-rays in order to exclude the other diseases associated with chest pain. The levels of total serum cholesterol, lactate dehydrogenase (LDH), creatine phosphokinase (CPK), and creatine kinase MB isozyme (CKMB) are determined within the first twenty-four hours, with three other CKMB studies also done. All these tests are for the quantitative evaluation of enzymes and fat residues, studies that assist in the diagnosis of acute myocardial infarction and assess the degree of damage to the heart muscle.

When the CKMB studies show elevated levels and the serial electrocardiograms demonstrate characteristic T-wave depressions, ST-segment elevations, and abnormal Q waves with or without irregular rhythms or bundle-branch blocks, the clinical diagnosis of acute myocardial infarction is considered to be proven. Tissue-plasminogen activator, an enzyme that helps remove blood clots, is then begun by intravenous injection. An echocardiogram, coronary-artery catheterization, and/or coronary angiography are also done when necessary to help determine the degree and type of acute myocardial infarction, and the location and extent of the arterial atherosclerosis and occlusion (blockage). In other words, as soon as a diagnosis of myocardial infarction is made, a substance is quickly given intravenously to help prevent the formation of blood clots in the arteries of the heart muscle. In some cases, further therapy, including coronary angioplasty or bypass grafts, is recommended. And if there is enough blockage in the coronary arteries, the patient is transferred by ambulance or helicopter to a heart center for open heart surgery. This very technical description is presented to show the high quality of care and treatment that is given to patients who are admitted to the intensive care unit of Titus County Memorial Hospital. The records and protocol are excellent and paved the way for me to complete an intensive epidemiological study on the use of vitamin B_6 before death caused by myocardial infarction.[1] (In an epidemiological study, researchers look at a certain segment of the population to determine the cause, incidence, and control of a certain disease.)

The time was right for my study. In 1995, the *New England Journal of Medicine* had reported for the first time an association between homocysteine and arterial atherosclerosis. Writing about carotid-artery operations, the authors of the article had concluded, "High plasma homocysteine concentrations and low concentrations of folate and vitamin B_6, through their role in homocysteine metabolism, are associated with an increased risk of extracranial carotid-artery stenosis in the elderly."[2] In effect, the article said that vitamin B_6 is the coenzyme of cystathionine synthase, the enzyme that converts homocysteine, an atherogenic amino acid, to cystathionine, a nonatherogenic amino acid. Today, this concept is widely accepted by the scientific community.[3,4] (For a complete discussion of vitamin B_6 and homocysteine, see page 91.)

My epidemiological study was important because of what happens every day and night in this nation. Coronary heart disease is the leading killer disease in the United States. Yet, for five years, from January 1, 1988, to January 1, 1992, the number of death certificates in Titus County showing myocardial infarction as the cause of death was 15.8-percent lower than the average number of such death certificates in each of the fourteen northeastern Texas counties including Titus. The rate of death from myocardial infarction in the sixty-to-sixty-nine age group in Titus County was 20.8-percent lower. In Titus County, with a population of 24,009 people, an estimated 1,500 people took supplemental vitamin B_6 daily during those years.

Vitamin B$_6$ and Homocysteine

It would seem logical that talking or writing about protein in meat, milk, cheese, eggs, and beans near the turn of the twenty-first century would be boring to an audience of distinguished people. But, exciting information exists. The protein in our bodies is composed of twenty amino acids. Nineteen of those amino acids are dependent on vitamin B$_6$ for their biochemical and metabolic functioning. Furthermore, when ingested, methionine, a sulfur-containing amino acid, is changed in the liver to homocysteine, a protein substance of far-reaching significance for the half a million American citizens who die each year from coronary heart disease.

Just under fifty years ago, in Belfast, Northern Ireland, two little girls were born with dislocated lenses in their eyes. These little Irish sisters became mentally retarded. Physicians and scientists found that the urine of these children contained an abnormal protein substance. This inherited disease condition was called homocystinuria. Both of the sisters died at early ages because of blood clots in their arteries. Post-mortem examinations revealed that both children had arteriosclerosis like old women.[5]

Biochemists at different American universities and at the National Institutes of Health (NIH) discovered that in these children with homocystinuria, the liver was unable to dispose of homocysteine in the normal fashion because of a genetic error in the liver enzyme cystathionine synthase. The NIH biochemists discovered that this enzyme normally converts homocysteine to cystathionine, which is then further processed in the liver to cysteine, another sulfur-containing amino-acid substance, and to sulfate for excretion in the urine. At about the same time, other researchers discovered that some patients with homocystinuria require vitamin B_6 in moderately large doses for the reduction of their high homocysteine levels. The conclusion was that systathionine synthase, the liver enzyme shown to be abnormal in homocystinuria, requires vitamin B_6 for normal activity. Moderately large doses of vitamin B_6 should therefore dramatically decrease the amount of homocysteine in the urine of these patients. This finding stimulated hundreds of physicians and scientists worldwide to study the biochemical and pathological relationship of vitamin B_6 to homocysteine.

Nineteen different amino acids in the human body are taken apart by more than a hundred enzymes, which require the assistance of vitamin B_6, a cofactor in the activities of these enzymes. For more than fifty years, scientists have been studying the function of vitamin B_6 in the liver, brain, blood, muscles, cartilage, bone, hormones, and, more recently, the arteries, large and small.

Arteriosclerosis has been associated with diabetes, aging, smoking, and the consumption of animal fats and cholesterol. However, scientists have recently begun debating the roles of fats and cholesterol in arteriosclerosis. Yes, animal fats and cholesterol do play roles, but the problems they cause are secondary and subsequent to the damage to the endothelial cells lining the arteries caused by excessive amounts of homocysteine circulating in the blood. Homocysteine also causes changes in the smooth muscle cells, elastin, and fibrous tissue in the walls of the arteries, as well as in the space between these elements. This space, known as the matrix, is where fats and cholesterol enter the picture. Cholesterol and fatty substances leak into the matrix, where the cholesterol, once oxygenated by blood, adds a thickness to the artery that is commonly identified as plaque. In other words, a deadly mixture of chemicals in the walls of the arteries leading to calcification and blockage of the blood going to the heart through the coronary arteries and to the brain through the carotid arteries in the neck has been found in association with high levels of homocysteine. Also of significance is the clotting of blood at the site of plaque in the carotid arteries. When one of these clots breaks loose, the result is stroke or paralysis. Vitamin B_6 helps prevent abnormal clotting of blood in the open lumen of arteries.

In the Non-invasive Cardiology Laboratory at New York University Medical Center, echographs done on 156 patients showed atherosclerosis in each thoracic aorta (the largest artery carrying blood from the heart). It was determined that high blood levels of homocysteine were positively correlated with the most severe cases of atherosclerosis in the thoracic aorta. It was also determined that these high homocysteine blood levels were accompanied by low vitamin-B_6 levels. In other words. it was proven at New York University Medical Center that high blood levels of homocysteine and low blood levels of vitamin B_6 contribute to severe calcification in the aortas of patients with advanced atherosclerosis.[6]

Biochemists have also found that two B vitamins are important in the chemistries of methionine. In something of a circle, so to speak, homocysteine is changed back into methionine by folic acid and vitamin B_{12}. But the main process of converting excess homocysteine to cystathione and then to cysteine and sulfate for excretion through the kidneys depends on vitamin B_6.

Homocysteine also plays a role in diabetes, acceptas a risk factor for both myocardial infarction and arteriosclerosis. In both diabetes mellitus type I and type II, arteriosclerosis can lead to heart attack, stroke, and leg amputation. It is now known that in the presence of kidney failure associated with diabetes, the blood level of homocysteine may be two to three times that of a normal person. It is also known that excessive sugar in the blood in some way lowers the vitamin-B$_6$ blood level. Furthermore, it is recognized that vitamin B$_6$ prevents, to a favorable degree, the abnormal union of blood sugar and proteins. In other words, vitamin B$_6$ prevents to an extent the abnormal union of protein substances with excess glucose in the blood of diabetic patients. This changes the whole concept of vitamin-B$_6$ therapy in diabetic patients. These patients need increased dosages of B$_6$ for protection.

As we approach the twenty-first century, we are entitled to ask, "What can our federal government do to help prevent arteriosclerosis and its associated deadly disease conditions?" The answer rests not only with the FDA and NIH, but also with the food industry. Vitamin B$_6$ and folic acid must be added to staple foods as supplements to assist in the maintenance of health in the United States of America throughout the coming century.

During the five-year study period, the patients with cardiac chest pain that I admitted to the intensive care unit numbered thirteen. In contrast, nine other physicians each admitted an average of fifty patients with cardiac chest pain. Among the patients I admitted having acute chest pain, almost all of whom had taken vitamin B$_6$ for more than one year, there was a marked reduction in the risk of myocardial infarction as compared to the patients with acute chest pain admitted by the other physicians. The conclusion was that vitamin B_6 helps in the prevention of myocardial infarction. Among my elderly patients who died of myocardial infarction at home or in a nursing home and had been taking vitamin B_6 for one to seventeen years, the average age at death was 84.5 years. Among the patients who had not taken vitamin B_6 or took it for less than one year, the average age at death was 76.7 years. Elderly people who had taken 100 to 200 milligrams of vitamin B_6 daily for long periods and died from myocardial infarction lived eight years longer than those who did not take vitamin B_6.

One case in particular in the study was very important. The patient was one of the thirteen I had admitted to the intensive care unit with acute myocardial infarction. In 1990, at the age of seventy-three, this man, who had taken 100 to 300 milligrams of vitamin B_6 per day for thirty-two years, had an acute myocardial infarction caused by the threat of attack by an intruder. Given tissue-plasminogen activator intravenously while in the intensive care unit, this elderly patient's cardiac catheterization showed a decreased perfusion of the lateral and inferior muscles of the heart. In plain language, the blood flow to the muscles of his heart had been reduced by blood clots in the tiny arteries going into the heart muscles. An angiograph showed that all of the large heart arteries were wide open and that there was no blockage in any of the heart arteries caused by calcified plaques or atherosclerosis. Remember, this man had been taking 100 to 300 milligrams of vitamin B_6 daily for a third of a century. A stress test administered later that year showed that his heart's normal ejection fraction (the percentage of blood forced out of the heart with each beat) at rest was 50 percent and at peak exercise was 70 percent. In 1998, at the age of eighty-one, this man was still in excellent condition.

What does this mean in plain language? This man had a stress heart attack. People have stress heart attacks from fear, excitement, or anger. This man lived over a stress heart attack. The fact that catheterization showed there was no blockage in the arteries going to the heart muscle was nothing less than exciting. The patient had no calcification in his heart arteries.

A splendid internist told me once that he had never seen a nondiabetic woman die of a heart attack before menopause. Cardiologists know that in some way, as yet unexplained, women are protected by their female hormones. Recent research indicates that a decrease in the production of the female sex hormones may cause an increase in the plasma-homocysteine levels. Some ten years after menopause, myocardial infarction becomes frequent. What are the biochemistries? How are they all connected? What does vitamin B_6 have to do with coronary heart disease? In short, vitamin B_6 must be present in adequate amounts for the proper movement and delivery of different vital trace substances and chemicals into and through the cells of different organs by way of the arteries, large and small. During pregnancy, different scientists have proven the umbilical-cord blood carrying nutrients to the developing fetus may have inadequate vitamin B_6. The mother is usually B_6 deficient and becomes more so after giving birth if she breastfeeds unless she takes adequate supplemental vitamin B_6. There are varying amounts of vitamin B_6 in human breast milk.[7]

Children are in jeopardy. Changes in the arteries begin in childhood, and in the presence of vitamin-B_6 deficiency, they include the loss of elastic fibrils in the walls of the arteries. The elastic fibrils are protected by hormones, but those hormones are moved into and out of the different tissues by enzymes dependent on vitamin B_6. The appropriate dosage of vitamin B_6 for children is currently the subject of much heated argument and open challenge. The answer depends on the child's age, weight, and general condition. It further depends on whether the child will be taking the B_6 indefinitely or for a limited period of time. Preschoolers can safely take 10 milligrams of vitamin B_6 daily. School-age children can take 50 milligrams daily. Normal teenagers, from age thirteen on, should take 100 milligrams of B_6 daily.

The critics ask, "Why are you so excited? Why do you think all of this vitamin B_6 is necessary?" The answer is that virtually all pregnant women are deficient in vitamin B_6, and in the presence of diabetes, there is an abnormal and pathological (disease-related) union of blood glucose with protein in different tissues. Furthermore, most untreated diabetics are deficient in vitamin B_6 because, in true circular fashion, hyperglycemia turns around and further drives down the B_6 blood level. This is the main reason that diabetes is such a serious risk factor for coronary heart disease. Because sixteen million Americans are diabetic and coronary heart disease is the leading killer disease in the United States, every diabetic should take the safe and proven dosage of 300 milligrams of vitamin B_6 daily.

Biochemists know that in the presence of vitamin B_6, most amino acids are degraded as a part of normal metabolism in a series of reactions or activities. In certain instances, the residues when a protein molecule is split but left unattended can become dangerously toxic. A number of scientists have shown that the incomplete degradation of tryptophan is associated with diabetes, and is probably a cause of the disease, certainly in some rats. Normal tryptophan degradation involves three enzymes that are dependent upon vitamin B_6. When degradation is incomplete because of a deficiency of B_6, the metabolites appear in the urine, and picolinate is not present in sufficient quantity for chelation and union with chromium.[8]

Recent research has shown that when the B vitamins folic acid, vitamin B_6, and vitamin B_{12} are low, there is improper degradation of methionine. The result is an excess of homocysteine, which is toxic and leads to arteriosclerosis and atherosclerosis. A combination of the biochemical failure of the degradation of methionine, lysine, and tryptophan can lead to a leakage of fluid, cholesterol, and fatty substances into the walls of the arteries in the eyes, which can lead to diabetic blindness. Vitamin B_6 must be present in adequate amounts for the normal degradation of tryptophan and methionine, and the prevention of the blinding and deadly disease conditions that affect millions of people in the United States.

In a study matching 304 patients with coronary heart disease to 231 healthy individuals, researchers at the Cleveland Clinic found the plasma-homocysteine levels to be higher in the heart-disease patients than in the healthy persons. They also found folic acid, previously the recommended therapy for patients with elevated plasma-homocysteine levels, to be present in higher amounts in the heart-disease patients than in the controls. They found no correlation between the elevated plasma-homocysteine levels and vitamin B_{12}. However, they did find low pyridoxal-phosphate levels in 10 percent of the heart-disease patients as compared to 2 percent of the controls.[9] The researchers concluded that within the range currently considered to be the norm, the risk for coronary heart disease rises along with the plasma-homocysteine level regardless of age or sex. And, in addition to a link with homocysteine, low pyridoxal phosphate "confers an independent risk for coronary artery disease," according to homocysteine researcher Dr. Killian Robinson and his associates.[10]

In his book *The Homocysteine Revolution*, pathologist Kilmer S. McCully described at length and in detail how homocysteine causes hardening of the arteries and calcification leading to arteriosclerosis. In effect, he said, there is increasing fibrosis (synthesis of excessive fibrous tissue) and loss of elasticity in the walls of the arteries, leading to heart attack or stroke. The homocysteine approach is radically different from the traditional view, which relates arteriosclerosis to the consumption of excess fat and cholesterol. Recent proof from many laboratories shows that through different biochemical activities, vitamin B_6, vitamin B_{12}, and folic acid all remove homocysteine from the bloodstream. In the scientific community and the medical profession, this constitutes the beginning of a revolution in the prevention and treatment of disease in the arteries of the heart, brain, and legs. The B-vitamin therapy goes beyond cholesterol.[11]

If ever there was a time marked by a spectacular gathering of conclusive information regarding the risk factors of heart attack, that time was November 1997. An article entitled "Homocysteine and Coronary Artery Disease," published in *The Archives of Internal Medicine*, the journal of the American Medical Association, was sent to 95,800 readers in seventy-eight countries. A total of 153 references were listed in the review, which concisely summarized the complex biochemistries and reviewed the cellular pathology in the walls of the arteries. Treatment with folic acid, vitamin B_6, and vitamin B_{12} was presented and explained.[12] Also in November 1997, physicians and scientists in the Department of Cardiology at the Cleveland Clinic published a comprehensive review entitled "Homocysteine: Update on a New Risk Factor" in the *Cleveland Clinic Journal of Medicine*.[13] In addition, the sixty-six tribes of Native Americans in Oklahoma responded to the medical data concerning homocysteine and the fact that diabetes is a risk factor of heart attacks. Years ago, the Trail of Tears brought the Choctaw tribe from Mississippi to Indian Territory. On November 7, 1997, the chief of the Choctaw spoke with dignitaries from southern Oklahoma in a meeting that resulted in the opening of the Choctaw Nation Diabetic Treatment Center in Antlers, Oklahoma, the first facility of its kind operated by a Native American tribe. November 1997 will be remembered in medical history.

Chapter 8

ARTHRITIS AND RHEUMATISM

Songs are written about the hands. Musicians need to be able to instantly move their fingers to play their instruments. The soft touch of love lingers long after the fingers have moved on. Such a simple organ, yet in reality, the hand is one of the most complicated anatomical structures of the body. It performs a multitude of movements, and houses the specialized tissues for those movements. And most often, it is never fully appreciated until pain and stiffness limit its flexibility.

While doing clinical research, I found men and women from different backgrounds and of various ages complaining of similar pain. They attributed their problems to "arthritis," "rheumatism," or "poor circulation," all of which are misleading, archaic, ambiguous terms because they in no way describe a specific disease process. One woman in her early forties complained of being unable to play a musical instrument because of painful finger joints, yet she didn't mention any tingling or numbness in her hands. Another woman exhibited the same symptoms, but she was in her early twenties and pregnant. Still another patient was a two-hundred-pound laborer whose hands had become crippled from what he termed "arthritis." "Neuritis," "bursitis," and "tendinitis" are all legitimate medical terms more meaningful than the general term "arthritis" that so many of my patients used.

To make a correct diagnosis, I had to take into consideration the neurological structure of the hand—that is, the different nerves in the hand and their relationships to the fingers. The median nerve supplies sensation to the thumb, index finger, middle finger, and inside of the ring finger, while the ulnar nerve supplies sensation to the adjacent sides of the ring and little fingers. (See Figure 4.1 on page 48.) I also had to take into consideration the finger joints, as well as the tendons and ligaments around the joints. Additionally, I had to look at the bones, muscles, cartilage, and blood vessels.

It was at this point that a mundane occurrence pointed me in the right direction. My neighbor's lawn mower gave up the ghost. And while telling me about it, my neighbor explained that the machine's nylon bearings had worn out and the motor had overheated, resulting in a number of its parts becoming fused together. "It was all that heat from the friction," my neighbor said sadly, on his way to buying a new mower. Heat . . . friction . . . nylon . . . bearings . . . The words stayed in my mind. Finally, it dawned on me that there was an element I had been overlooking, simply because I hadn't realized its importance. It was a revelation not unlike the one about arteriosclerosis prompted by the plumber's visit. I had been concentrating on the basic parts of the hand, forgetting that there is a vital element without which everything could fuse together, similar to what happened to my neighbor's lawn mower. That element was synovium.

Synovium is the paper-thin, almost transparent, slippery layer of tissue that surrounds the tendons and allows them to move without friction. Synovium might be called the body's built-in lubrication system, and is part of every joint in the knee, elbow, shoulder, hip, and, of course, the hand. (See Figure 4.3 on page 52, as well as Figures 8.1 and 8.2.) Without synovium, the constant friction might well make the

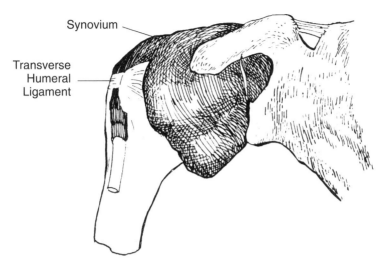

Figure 8.1. Right shoulder joint.

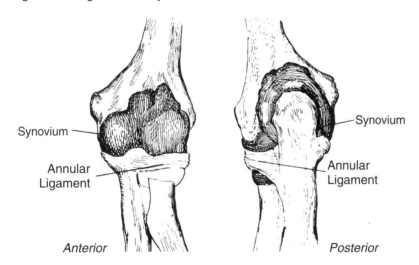

Figure 8.2. Anterior and posterior elbow joints.

hand's components become overheated. I remembered the woman who could not play the musical instrument because of stiffness and pain in her hands. Playing a piano or violin, for example, would place more than the normal amount of strain on the fingers and joints, and without synovium, the heat buildup would undoubtedly become unbearable.

A joint is made more stable for bearing weight not only by the cartilage inside it, but also by the synovium outside and surrounding it. Cartilage receives its nutrition from synovium, in the form of water, long-chain sugars, vitamin C, and sulfated proteins. Cartilage has no nerves, arteries, veins, or lymphatics, while synovium has all of these. The pain of soft-tissue rheumatism therefore begins in synovium, which has nerves, and not in cartilage, which does not have nerves.[1]

We now know that a number of disease conditions are linked to, associated with, or the result of sustained vitamin-B_6 deficiency. Most of what people term "arthritis" or "rheumatism" can be traced to a number of these conditions, including carpal tunnel syndrome; acute, subacute, and chronic noninflammatory tenosynovitis (inflammation of a tendon sheath due to a biochemical change in the cells rather than pus or a bacterial infection); acute, subacute, and chronic noninflammatory tendinitis (inflammation of a tendon due to a biochemical change in the cells rather than pus or a bacterial infection); DeQuervain's disease (synovitis of the thumb tendons); diabetes mellitus; diabetic neuropathy as related to carpal tunnel syndrome; periarticular synovitis (inflammation of the synovium around multiple joints); shoulder-hand syndrome (severe pain, stiffness, and loss of movement in the entire arm, from the shoulder to the hand and including all the joints in between); premenstrual edema; menopausal arthritis; pregnancy-related edema; pregnancy-induced hypertension; the use of birth control pills; arterial subendothelial proliferation (an increase in the smooth muscle cells, foam cells, fibers, and connective tissues in the walls of arteries); and arteriosclerosis.[2]

Patients with a form of arthritis known as degenerative osteoarthritis, particularly in the finger joints, around the shoulders, and around the knees, also respond to vitamin-B_6 therapy, primarily in the early stages or as a preventive. (See Figures 8.3 and 8.4.) No amount of B_6 will reverse or improve extremely advanced degenerative osteoarthritis. Heberden's

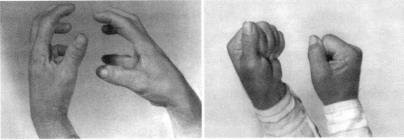

Flexion before   Flexion after

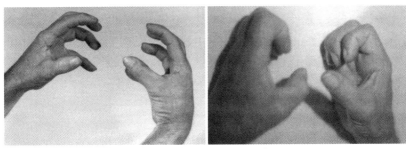

Flexion before   Flexion after

Figure 8.3. Flexion of hands before and after treatment with vitamin B_6.

nodes (small, hard, painful nodules at the distal finger joints) are considered a part of osteoarthritis and, in most cases, respond to 200 milligrams of vitamin B_6 taken daily, with any nodules remaining after treatment no longer painful to the touch or pressure. However, there is an age relationship. Older patients show only partial improvement in their symptoms of rheumatism and osteoarthritis. But the degree of lasting improvement warrants further investigation and study of the effects of long-term treatment with vitamin B_6.

Biochemist Stephen Coburn, writing in the August 1985 edition of *Better Nutrition*, considered long-term treatment with vitamin B_6 in light of the laboratory data on B_6 deficiency. In his article, he reported that there are two pools of vitamin B_6—the *pool short*, the supply of vitamin B_6 that is dissolved in the blood plasma and can rise or drop in a matter of hours; and the *pool long*, the supply of B_6 that is stored 80-percent in

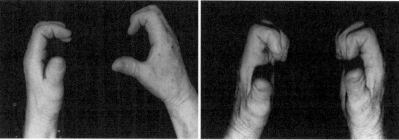

Flexion of hands before   Flexion of hands after

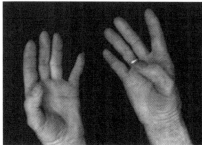

Flexion of thumbs before   Flexion of thumbs after

Figure 8.4. Flexion of hands and thumbs before and after treatment with vitamin B_6.

the muscles and 20-percent in the liver, and can remain at a constant level for several weeks.[3] In other words, a patient might test deficient one day, but not the next. Pool-short plasma levels can change in a matter of hours, while pool-long plasma levels may not show any significant change for days.

Scientists have conducted extensive research on the cartilage in the joints and elastin in the aortas of chickens. Cartilage is the rather firm, elastic, fibrous substance that in humans is part of the skeleton inside some joints and part of other joints such as the knee, hip, and elbow. It is composed of a number of fibers and cells including collagen fibrils for strength, elastic fibrils for elasticity, and reticular fibrils for support, all imbedded in a matrix that serves as a framework to hold everything together. Elastin is similar to collagen and is the primary component of elastic fibrils. According to the research with chickens, the amino acid lysine must have the enzyme lysyl oxidase present for the protection of the strong cross-links between the collagen fibrils in cartilage and the elastic fibrils in aortas. When vitamin B_6 was given to young chickens deficient in that nutrient, the result was a marked and favorable increase in the lysyl-oxidase levels in both the cartilage and the aorta. Vitamin B_6 was proven to be a cofactor of lysyl oxidase.[4] The researchers further found, with the help of a microscope, that in the chickens' ankle joints, just above the claws, the collagen fibrils in the cartilage were spread apart, swollen, and reduced in number.[5] This is the strongest evidence yet that prolonged vitamin-B_6 deficiency in humans causes crippling in the joints, the knees in particular, and changes in the aortas, which as a result become subject to aneurysms.

A surgeon who operates on hands for carpal tunnel syndrome told me that in some patients, the tendons in the hand seem to be swollen; in other patients, the synovium is swollen; and in still other patients, there is a dense thickening of the transverse ligament in the carpal tunnel. (See Figure 4.3 on page 52.) All of these conditions contribute to the pressure on the median nerve at the carpal tunnel. (See Figure 4.1 on page 48.) In some way, to some extent, vitamin B_6 reverses all these changes. Following treatment with vitamin B_6 over a period of ninety days, the muscles contracting in the forearm stimulated movement of the tendons to allow normal flexion of the fingers at the joints.[6]

In other research, D.M. Yamaguchi, P.R. Lipscomb, and E.H. Soule analyzed the data from 1,215 cases of carpal tunnel syndrome treated at the Mayo Clinic over a period of thirty years and found that 121 of the patients had periarthritis of the shoulder (subdeltoid bursitis, bicipital tendinitis, calcific tendinitis, or adhesive capsulitis).[7] In a review of 818 cases of carpal tunnel syndrome treated at the Cleveland Clinic over a period of twenty-one years, Dr. George Phalen reported that DeQuervain's disease and periarticular arthritis of the finger joints frequently accompanied carpal tunnel syndrome.[8] In a study I conducted, patients treated with vitamin B_6 had definite improvement of the periarticular arthritis of their fingers as exhibited by a reduction in the swelling, pain, and stiffness around the interphalangeal joints. The reduction in the pain in the extensor tendons of the thumb caused by the DeQuervain's disease was particularly spectacular and enduring in two patients who continued to take vitamin B_6 for eight years. In some cases, a reduction in the pain in the rotary and bicipital tendons around the shoulders followed treatment with vitamin B_6.[9] A number of different forms of rheumatism may now be re-evaluated based on this successful treatment of carpal tunnel syndrome with vitamin B_6.

The term "menopausal arthritis" is commonly accepted and used by physicians, particularly rheumatologists. Menopausal arthritis is a form of arthritis experienced by women beginning around the time of menopause. Research has proven that when the blood-estrogen level decreases, vitamin-B_6 intake must be increased to ensure the complete metabolism of the essential amino acid tryptophan.[10] Following menopause, there is a reduction in steroid-hormone activity. To offset this, the adrenal glands produce a lower quantity of their hormones. The vitamin-B_6 level therefore also declines in the body, causing menopausal arthritis on a quantitative basis. To prevent or cure menopausal arthritis, adequate vitamin B_6 must be present to facilitate normal steroid-hormone activity. One of my patients developed increasing stiffness, pain, and swelling in her fingers at the age of forty-eight, about the time she ceased menstruating. The symptoms worsened over the years, and the woman would soak her hands in warm water in an effort to obtain some relief. She took pain medication, but enjoyed only partial and temporary relief. This menopausal arthritis in her fingers and hands troubled the woman for some fifteen years. When the woman finally came to me for treatment, I prescribed 100 milligrams of vitamin B_6 daily. In ninety days, the patient still had some deformity in her finger joints, but all the swelling and pain had subsided. During the next twelve years, the woman's hands were comfortable and free of pain. The flexion in her fingers returned almost to normal. In my opinion, there are hundreds of thousands of women who are now taking highly advertised pain medication, but should take vitamin B_6.

Other patients experience pain and discomfort that is more vague, particularly around the neck and radiating downward to the shoulder. As one woman said, "Before taking vitamin B_6, I could not turn my head to the right and look over my shoulder. For months I experienced that pain. But after taking the vitamin B_6, I was able to look over my right shoulder without pain and easily back my car out of the garage."

The term "arthritis" is very broad and includes a number of conditions that are unrelated. Bacterial infections, gout, and rheumatoid arthritis are examples. Lupus erythematosis can cause swelling and pain in the hands and fingers almost identical to that caused by vitamin-B_6 deficiency. In like manner, rheumatoid arthritis can cause pain in the hands and fingers similar to, but not the same as, the crippling caused by B_6 deficiency. It has been my experience that a patient can have two conditions at the same time, and that the proper treatment approach is to prescribe 200 milligrams of vitamin B_6 daily for ninety days and then make another evaluation. If any of the signs or symptoms have improved, the 200 milligrams of B_6 should be continued indefinitely.

As a result of my research, I firmly believe that 90 percent of what is called arthritis in the United States is, in reality, a biochemical change in the synovium of the tendons and joints, particularly in the fingers, thumbs, elbows, shoulders, knees, and hips. The epidemic incidence of B_6 deficiency today is the root cause. With changes in the synovium, a person experiences swelling, pain, and stiffness in the joints, symptoms that most men and women, including doctors, call "arthritis."[11]

Today's modern diet is high in protein, supplied largely by meat, chicken, milk, cheese, eggs, and fish. Vitamin B_6 must be available in adequate amounts in order for the enzymes to be broken apart and for the body to utilize the different amino acids from the protein. If B_6 is lacking, the metabolites that result may be toxic. For example, with a vitamin-B_6 deficiency, there is an abnormal buildup in the blood of 3-hydroxy-kynurenine and 3-hydroxyanthranilic acid, metabolites of tryptophan. These metabolites suppress the production of insulin by the pancreas.[12] Methionine, also rich in beef, cheese, chicken, cooked eggs, peanut butter, and plain yogurt, becomes toxic in the presence of a vitamin-B_6 deficiency. It has been proven that homocysteine, which is a metabolite of methionine, must be further broken down by an enzyme in the human body that is dependent on B_6.[13]

By now we can see a new dimension to the aging process in the United States. Diabetes, arteriosclerosis, myocardial infarction, and soft-tissue rheumatism are not necessarily the result of aging, but in different ways relate to vitamin-B_6 deficiency. Here again is that delicate relationship between the hormones that gradually decline through the years. The reduction in the quantities of hormones makes it all the more essential that adequate vitamin B_6 be taken daily to ensure the efficient movement of the hormones into the different skeletal tissues in and around the joints. This reduces pain and crippling in aged people.

Chapter 9

BRAIN FUNCTION

More than ten billion nerve cells in the human brain hold the keys to how we think, feel, learn, remember, move, and sense the world around us. These nerve cells, called neurons, are the brain's basic building blocks. Researchers are discovering something new about neurons and the workings of the brain every day.

When we touch something, the impulse speeds along a nerve network from the finger to the brain at roughly 350 feet per second. Even heavy-footed teenage drivers are incapable of speed like that. As scientists continue to refine brain-mapping techniques, it becomes easier to determine which section of the brain responds in any given situation. The brain is the most highly organized bit of matter in the universe. Since humans first became aware of its existence, they have struggled to comprehend the miracles and miseries dished out by this three-pound handful of cells. Their goals then and now have been the same—to gain a true understanding of how the brain works and to use that knowledge to improve the quality of life. So it seems to me that inception is a good time to begin making sure a child is properly brain-fed.

Between 1961 and 1973, I delivered 225 babies whose mothers had been given 50 to 450 milligrams of vitamin B$_6$ daily during pregnancy. One of the infants, DS, was born a fraternal twin of a mother who had demonstrated a high degree of edema during pregnancy. Luckily, the edema had responded to vitamin B$_6$. However, by eight months of age, DS had not developed normally. She would not hold a bottle or reach for one. Her mother had to feed her by holding her in her lap. The baby had no desire to crawl. It was impossible to get her to grasp and hold a baby rattle, spoon, or any other object. In addition, she had convulsions whenever she experienced any elevation of temperature. I prescribed 12 milligrams of vitamin B$_6$ by mouth daily. Within one week, DS was attempting to crawl in her crib, playing, clutching objects, and shaking her baby rattle vigorously and with good coordination. She held her bottle herself while drinking from it. It was a striking change.

Subsequently, DS was diagnosed with epilepsy. She was treated with 50 milligrams daily of vitamin B$_6$, along with Dilantin, a medication used in the treatment of epilepsy. A glucose tolerance test showed that her blood sugar was within the normal range.

DS grew into a pretty little girl. She could talk, had a nice smile, liked to draw pictures with coloring pencils, and seemed happy, but she had to be placed in special education in school. At thirty years of age, she was friendly and still had her nice smile, but she was, to a degree, mentally retarded.

TG, another infant I delivered, also required an increased amount of vitamin B$_6$. TG was born preterm of a mother who was nineteen years old and pregnant for the first time. During the mother's first prenatal visit, I prescribed a multi-vitamin-and-mineral supplement containing nine vitamins and six minerals. Each capsule included 10 milligrams of vitamin B$_6$, but only 1 milligram of magnesium sulfate. Two months later, I added an additional 50 milligrams of vitamin B$_6$ to the daily regime, but the young mother-to-be, of her own accord, discontinued taking the added B$_6$. Thirty days later, the young woman developed toxemia of pregnancy with extensive edema in her hands and feet. When she began taking 100 milligrams of vitamin B$_6$ daily along with the multivitamin-and-mineral supplement, the edema subsided. Her blood pressure remained high, however, and at the time of delivery was 182 over 120. This was true toxemia of pregnancy.

The baby, TG, weighed three pounds fourteen ounces at birth, which put him in the preterm classification. He was placed in an incubator. As was the accepted custom in caring for preterm infants, one-fourth ounce of 5-percent glucose was given to TG at two-hour intervals for seven feedings, beginning twenty-eight hours after birth. Eighty-one hours after birth, TG began having convulsions in the incubator. I administered 25 milligrams of vitamin B$_6$ by intramuscular injection. The convulsions promptly ceased. Three and a half years later, TG was admitted to a Ft. Worth hospital with extremely low blood sugar. An electroencephalogram suggested that he had a convulsive disorder. TG had continued to have convulsive seizures over the years, but had not been given vitamin B$_6$. At my suggestion, his mother gave him 25 milligrams of vitamin B$_6$ daily over the next year and 50 milligrams daily over the following four years. During this period, TG had no more convulsive seizures.

Shortly after his first-grade year in school and following his parent's divorce, TG became withdrawn and uncommunicative. He failed second grade and was not promoted to third grade. A glucose tolerance test administered that year showed he had a "flat sugar tolerance curve except for a low level of 45 milligrams percent at three hours." Milligrams percent is the laboratory unit of measurement used to indicate blood-sugar levels in humans. It can vary hour to hour depending on what the person has eaten. On the basis of TG's glucose tolerance test, his history of convulsions in the incubator following the oral administration of glucose, and his low blood-sugar levels found by two laboratories at different times, I diagnosed TG as having reactive hypoglycemia—that is, his blood sugar at times tended to dip very low. TG had proven responsive to vitamin B_6, but he also had displayed a blood-sugar disorder. His body was having a problem metabolizing sugar and other refined carbohydrates. Here again was a confusing relationship between abnormal sugar metabolism and an increased need for vitamin B_6 in a child who had been born preterm.

I advised TG's mother to continue giving her son 50 milligrams of vitamin B_6 daily, plus I recommended a high-protein, medium-fat, low-carbohydrate diet. In a follow-up visit, the mother stated, "[TG] is doing well since you put him on that diet. Before the diet, he sat around as if he had no energy. His teacher said he is so different at school that she even had to scold him a couple of times because he was 'picking' at other children, something he has never done in the past."

A few days later, I telephoned TG's teacher for confirmation. Iona Carpenter was a highly skilled professional with master's degrees in elementary education and the psychology of exceptional children. Over the previous seven years, this teacher had taught reading and spelling to about two hundred children with dyslexia, a learning disorder marked by an impaired ability to recognize or comprehend written words. Mrs. Carpenter said, "Before beginning treatment with the special [high-protein, medium-fat, low-carbohydrate] diet, TG would sit in his seat withdrawn from all around him, as if he were dreaming all by himself. He had no interest in schoolwork, and it was difficult to hold his attention. He frowned all the time. His movements were slow, coordination was poor, and he seemed to have little energy. I had to stand in the door to wait for him to arrive to begin nearly every class." Since starting the special diet, Mrs. Carpenter reported, "[TG] pays attention, arrives at class on time and coordination in his movement has improved and he now walks faster. There has been a definite improvement in work habits and his reading skills. He even asked for a new reader to take home. He talks to children around him and laughs now, whereas before he appeared not to really care about life."

Some very important and lasting information was provided by TG's case. TG was born preterm of a teenaged mother who suffered from toxemia of pregnancy including pregnancy-related edema. The edema had responded to the vitamin-B_6 therapy, but the high blood pressure had not. Both conditions are complications of toxemia of pregnancy. After birth, TG responded to vitamin B_6 when he suffered convulsions in the incubator and again at age three. Between the ages of three and eight, he was given 25 to 50 milligrams of vitamin B_6 daily and had no more convulsions, even though he survived on a diet that included candy, cookies, carbonated drinks, and ice cream almost daily. I believe that the most important factor in TG's case was his dietary imbalance. His body either could not tolerate a high-carbohydrate diet or needed a high amount of protein to supply something he hadn't been getting. TG also needed more vitamin B_6 than his peers. The results obtained from placing TG on a proper diet were little short of incredible. The dietary improvement changed his mood from one of frustration and despair to that of accomplishment and zest for life. At the age of thirty-three, TG was not diabetic, did not have convulsive seizures, and was actively employed. My conclusion was that all hypoglycemics should take vitamin B_6 as a supplement in addition to consuming a diet individualized to the particular patient.

The cases of DS and TG opened the way for my very serious study of brain function in infants and children. For decades, it has been known that the amino acid tryptophan, found in meat, fish, chicken, eggs, and milk, requires vitamin B_6 for its proper biochemical breakdown. From tryptophan, there are four pathways of biochemical degradation, which result in the formation of some twenty different metabolites or substances that are either useful to the body or must be excreted as waste products through the kidneys. The primary pathway leads to the formation of vitamin B_3. In other words, vitamin B$_6$ helps enzymes to form vitamin B$_3$, the antipellagra vitamin.

Another pathway of tryptophan degradation leads to the formation of serotonin.[1] In the brain, serotonin serves as a neurotransmitter. A neurotransmitter is a chemical substance that assists in the transmission of nerve impulses through the brain. Serotonin helps to regulate the sleep cycle and combats depression. Vitamin B$_6$ is a coenzyme that aids in the metabolism of serotonin and other neurotransmitters such as dopamine.

In children born with Down syndrome, serotonin is depressed in the central nervous system. In a study conducted by Mary Coleman of the Georgetown University School of Medicine in Washington, D.C., when vitamin B$_6$ was given to a number of infants with Down syndrome, there was an elevation of the whole-blood level of serotonin, particularly during the first eighteen months.[2] Although it did not have any clinically beneficial effects on growth and development, the vitamin-B$_6$ treatment was found to improve central-nervous-system functions, as evidenced by the infants' improved responses to voices and different noises.

Extensive studies have also been done on infantile autism, a behavioral syndrome consisting of specific disturbances in social relating and communication, language, response to objects, sensory modulation, and mobility, with an onset prior to thirty months of age. In autistic withdrawal, children seek to be alone, lack an interest in other people, have an aversion to affection and physical contact, and do not make eye contact. Autistic children often display gross defects in language, inappropriate facial expressions and gestures, unexplained screaming and laughing, and a peculiar interest in or attachment to objects such as dolls. Also, they have attention problems—for example, they are easily distracted, don't seem to listen, and don't seem to understand.

Among the early studies of the relationship of vitamin B$_6$ to autism is the work of Bernard Rimland, Ph.D., director of the Institute for Child Behavior Research in San Diego. In 1978, following the completion of a double-blind crossover study on the effects of high doses of vitamin B_6 on autistic children, he published his findings in an article in the *American Journal of Psychiatry*.[3] Additional studies were done by scientists at a university in France collaborating with scientists at the University of California at San Francisco and presented to the Third International Conference on Vitamin B_6, held in Goslar-Hahnenklee, Germany, in August 1987.[4] According to these studies, the best results without doubt were obtained when vitamin B_6 and magnesium were given together to autistic children. Vitamin B_6 and magnesium are cofactors in many brain functions. They help the neurotransmitters including serotonin to work more effectively. Most biochemical studies of autism have focused on the neurotransmitters in the brain and their metabolism. There is evidence that the metabolites of the neurotransmitters serotonin and dopamine are present in high levels in the spinal fluid, blood, and urine of autistic children.[5,6]

In the study conducted by Dr. Rimland, vitamin B_6 and magnesium were given to forty-four institutionalized children with a mean age of 9.3 years. The attending nurses of the children noted that fifteen (34 percent) showed improvement including better social behavior, increased alertness, reduced negativism, and reduced tantrums. In a review of scientific articles by researchers C. Barthelemy, J. Martineau, and associates, a total of ninety-one children with autism were discussed. Of these children, 14 percent responded to treatment with vitamin B_6 and magnesium, 33 percent showed improvement, 42 percent did not show improvement, and 11 percent became worse. The more responsive children were the younger ones.

According to a report by Dr. Rimland on his study, most of the children were given 300 to 500 milligrams of B_6 daily. The children were also given several hundred milligrams a day of magnesium as well as a vitamin-B-complex supplement to guard against B_6-induced deficiencies of these other nutrients. People vary enormously in their need for B_6, and Dr. Rimland noted, "The children who showed improvement under B_6 improved because they needed extra B_6. Autism is thus in many cases a vitamin B_6 dependency syndrome." While no autistic patient has been cured with vitamin B_6 and magnesium, many have shown remarkable improvement, including an eighteen-year-old who was considered too violent and assaultive to be kept in a hospital. As a last resort, the young man was given B_6 and magnesium. He calmed down into an easy-going person who sang and played guitar for his psychiatrist.[7]

Although hyperactivity is a severe problem with many autistic children, at a recent meeting in Fullerton, California, mothers, grade-school special-education teachers, and a clinical psychologist all concerned with hyperactive children concluded that hyperactivity in children is separate and apart from autism. Hyperactivity remains to a degree irreversible, even in adults. Infants born to malnourished mothers show a higher percentage of attention deficit hyperactivity disorder. Vitamin B_6 helps to normalize body metabolism, normalize brain waves and urine chemistry, and improve behavior.

As I mentioned at the start of this chapter, from 1962 to 1973, as part of my family practice, I prescribed 50 to 200 milligrams of vitamin B_6 as a daily supplement for 225 pregnant women. I observed both the mothers and infants before and after birth.[8] The only cases of abnormal brain function in an infant were observed in DS and TG. Based on my follow-up observations, I formed the opinion that when women take adequate vitamin B_6 during pregnancy and lactation, their children can recite nursery rhymes at very early ages. As these children grow, they become intelligent and valuable citizens. Some of "my" babies even became distinguished mathematicians.

In 1953, nervous irritability and convulsive seizures were reported in several hundred infants aged six weeks to six months.[9] An investigation indicated that the infants had been fed a commercial infant formula that had been heated twice, thus destroying much of its vitamin-B_6 content. (For a complete discussion of this case, see page 38.) This was the first time in medical history that vitamin B_6 was proven to be essential to the normal functioning of the human body. It was shown, in fact, to be essential to brain function and life itself. Sadly, it was later determined that some of the affected babies remained mentally retarded. Subsequent investigations revealed that substances transmitting light, sound, and heat in the brain are dependent on vitamin B_6.

How far is it from the eye of a hawk to its brain, and where in the human brain is emotion housed? The brain contains numerous specialized neurons grouped in specific regions to perform specific functions. Therefore, a whole-brain analysis cannot provide the information needed regarding the neurological disorders of vitamin-B_6 deficiency. Studies done with rat pups at Purdue University do show, however, that severe deficiency of vitamin B_6 in utero resulted in a 1,500-percent increase in shrunken neuron cells. If the study had been extended, the number of prematurely dying neurons conceivably would have increased progressively with age. These findings show clearly that "vitamin B_6 adequacy is essential to the normal morphological development of three brain regions: neocortex, caudate/putamen, and cerebellum."[10]

In summary, the brain abnormalities related to vitamin-B_6 deficiency include convulsive seizures, mental retardation, Down syndrome, autism, hypoglycemia, mental depression, and brain-cell damage in rats depleted of vitamin B_6, discussed in this chapter, as well as hyperglycemia, discussed in previous chapters. In different ways, all of these conditions indicate an increased need for vitamin B_6.

Chapter 10

DIETARY FACTORS INVOLVING VITAMIN B$_6$

In the early 1960s, I found myself growing accustomed to peeking through oxygen tents at ghastly pale patients in shock, their faces covered with cold, clammy sweat. I determined to find some way to change the trend that, both nationally and in my own practice, was becoming an epidemic. Although others, especially in laboratories, were undoubtedly working on various aspects of vitamin-B$_6$ research, I was unaware of their efforts in 1961, when this heightened concern over heart disease in my patients drove me to become involved in my own clinical research.

At the time, many researchers believed that they had found the major cause of heart disease—cholesterol. And they thought this belief was substantiated by the prominent role of saturated fats in the American diet. But, the controversy was far from one-sided. A bombardment of medical claims bolstered first one side, then the other. Certainly, cutting down drastically on saturated fats in the diet seemed a logical, sensible approach. Nothing alters a person's body more than the food he or she eats. Food has both direct and indirect bearing on health, depending on the quality, quantity, and kind of food eaten. The role of fat metabolism was a logical factor to consider in heart disease, as the American diet was composed of nearly 50-percent fats.

Having read the work of Dr. Ancel Keys, I began a study of the American diet. Dr. Keys was the director of the Laboratory of Physiological Hygiene at the University of Minnesota. He was the man for whom the famed K-ration of World War II had been named. His primary interest was fat and cholesterol. After analyzing several diets, I selected a low-fat diet developed by Dr. Lester M. Morrison at the College of Medical Evangelists in Los Angeles. Dr. Morrison had reported in the *Journal of the American Medical Association* that he had used the diet to successfully treat victims of coronary thrombosis.[1] Essentially, the diet substituted lean meat for fatty meat and increased the percentage of vegetables and fruits. It used vegetable oils for cooking instead of saturated fats of animal origin. It also seemed to supply balanced amounts of the vitamins and minerals.

My first patient on the Morrison diet was, in a way, my first patient in what ultimately became my clinical work with vitamin B₆. He was a tall, ruddy-faced, 210-pound oil-field worker. At fifty-five, this man outwardly appeared to be in the best of health. But that day, he didn't know whether he was, as he expressed it, "sick or crazy." His hands and arms tingled, and had for several months. He said it felt like waves of electricity were going up and down his arms and into his chest. When I asked him my diagnostic questions, he noted that he had cramps in his legs after going to bed. In addition, when I examined him, I noticed that the veins and tendons on the backs of his hands were not visible, suggesting a slight edema, but at the time, I did not assign much significance to this.

The oil-field worker had been consuming a diet high in cholesterol and seemed to be an ideal candidate for the low-fat Morrison diet. When he returned to my office in two weeks, his original symptoms had disappeared, but he now had pain in his shoulders and elbows. The low-fat diet had helped, but it had not restored him to complete health. On his third visit, though, the oil-field worker reported a change that impressed both of us. He had lost eight pounds and three inches off his waistline without attempting to do so! He had not cut down on his food intake, for I had not emphasized counting calories or measuring food. I felt it was more important to secure my patients' cooperation in eating the types of food the Morrison diet recommended than in eating specific amounts of the foods.

The evidence accumulated swiftly. A forty-year-old woman I had known since high school, whose deep freezer was filled with pork sausage, ham, and bacon, complained of muscle spasms in her feet at night that brought tears to her eyes. After thirty-six hours on the Morrison diet, she became symptom-free.

A seventy-year-old woman suffering from severe tingling, cramps, fainting, vertigo, and painful elbows and shoulders came in with a serum cholesterol level of 311 milligrams percent—quite high. The normal is 150 to 250 milligrams. On the Morrison diet, her tingling paresthesia, muscle spasms, fainting, and vertigo vanished, and her elbow-shoulder pain gradually improved. At one office visit, she blurted out, "If I knew how to play a piano, I could." Her words intrigued me long afterward. There was more involved than merely an absence of fats. This woman, as well as the other patients, was getting something extra from the diet, something that was not there before. What positive factor had restored this woman's finger function almost overnight? The answers to these questions clearly lay in the diet, but how could I pinpoint the specific factor?

Gradually I realized that the medical profession was blocked from final positive proof that excessive consumption of saturated fats alone causes coronary thrombosis. Each time the epidemiologists thought they had the solution, somebody like the Eskimos popped up. The Eskimos at that time had little heart disease, yet they ate blubber, which probably made their diet the highest in saturated fats. By then, I also realized that my patients had not eaten balanced diets before the Morrison diet and that the Morrison diet was high in vitamins and minerals. Many of my patients had even eaten diets that were more than 50-percent fats. When a person eats the fat from a steak, he or she gets no minerals, no vitamins, no enzymes, no nutrients— just calories. Fat calories are as "empty" as sugar calories. A diet composed of 50-percent fats means a diet the half of which does not provide proper nutrition.[2]

The fat-eater is as bad off in most ways as the alcoholic. When alcohol displaces food, the result is vitamin deficiencies. The same severe deficiencies may develop as a result of obtaining calories primarily from fat. Additionally, a high-fat diet may lead to obesity, for dietary fat must be converted into either energy, body fat, or waste. The arithmetic is simple. There are nine calories to a gram of fat and four to a gram of protein. It doesn't take many servings of fat to add up to a gain in weight.

My first progress in nailing down the most beneficial ingredient in the Morrison diet came, as often happens for a doctor, through another patient. In my case, this other patient was a man, a bachelor teacher in his sixties, who had come in for a regular physical examination. This man was free of symptoms and seemed to be enjoying such glowing health that I marveled at his suntan, still retained in the depth of winter, and at his general appearance. I asked about his diet. For the past eighteen months, he said, he had been eating pecans every day and cooking with peanut oil because of a diet he had heard about. Everything else in his diet was as it always had been. Could he tell a difference, I asked him. Yes, he said. For forty-five years, he had had pain in his knees every night after retiring. Now the pain was gone. His grip was also stronger, and his fingers were more limber, more flexible, not "stiff or fat," he said. Again, some dietary factor was at work, and it seemed to be in the pecans or peanuts.

A few days later, a sixty-six-year-old woman who had been hospitalized for diabetes and chest pain came in for a follow-up examination. She required fifty units of insulin daily to keep her blood sugar from going too high. I put her on the Morrison diet, with diabetic modifications. I also told her to eat peanuts and pecans each day. In two weeks, she had "just a little bit" of chest pain, which was a great improvement. Her fingers had been hurting, but now only one did. Her fingers were no longer stiff, and she could do her work.

This diabetic woman's case was more than just casually interesting. Sixteen years before, the woman had had a leg amputated above the knee because of bone cancer. For five years, she had been on a controlled diabetic diet. For several years, she had had tingling in her hands and cramping in one leg. Now, after two weeks on the Morrison diet supplemented by pecans and peanuts, those symptoms were gone, and as a bonus, the woman added, "I just feel better than I have felt in years."

Again, why? What, specifically, had changed this woman's health so suddenly? After much thought, I decided to investigate the B-complex vitamins. Undoubtedly, my patients had been getting the B vitamins in the Morrison diet, and the vitamin-B deficiencies produced a broad spectrum of disease conditions. I would start by working with five of the B vitamins—vitamin B$_1$, (thiamine), vitamin B$_2$ (riboflavin), vitamin B$_3$ (niacin), pantothenic acid, and vitamin B$_6$ (pyridoxine). If these vitamins produced the same results the diet had, my search would be narrowed. On the other hand, if these five vitamins did not materially alleviate the symptoms in question, I could rule them out and continue the search with other nutrients. To have a comparison point for the tests, I selected one symptom—paresthesia—that would serve as a point of reference with past, present, and future patients.

A successful dairyman in his fifties was the first patient who qualified for this second phase of my study. The man had a full range of symptoms, and he felt miserable. After unloading a truckload of hay the day before, he had suffered a pain in his chest and tingling in his hands and arms. His left arm had cramped. The aches and pains had kept him awake nearly all night. After administering an electrocardiogram and ruling out coronary thrombosis, I took the man into my confidence about the B-complex therapy. I explained to him that the symptoms might be related to heart disease and that I wanted to see if an injection of vitamins would help him. It is believed that some patients do not absorb vitamins properly from the intestines. Injection is the surest way of administering the B vitamins. "If it won't kill me and will help science, I'm ready to do it," the dairyman agreed.

I asked my wife, Lucy, a commercial artist whose work illustrates this book, to sketch the patient's hands in order to have an objective before-and-after record of the therapy. The man flexed the two joints of his fingers as much as he could while Lucy drew his hand exactly as she saw it. (See Figure 1 on page 7.) The man was unable to flex his fingers completely to the palm. The space between his fingertip and palm was large enough to accommodate a jumbo pencil.

Then, that day and every second day thereafter, I gave the man an arm-muscle injection containing 100 milligrams of vitamin B$_1$, 9.5 milligrams of vitamin B$_2$, 150 milligrams of vitamin B$_3$, 5 milligrams of panthenol, and 50 milligrams of vitamin B$_6$. At the end of two weeks, Lucy drew the man's hands again. Now he could flex his hands completely, pressing his fingertips into his palms. The B-complex injections had done the same as the Morrison diet, pecans, and peanuts had done.

One case can mean a lot. It also, for reasons at first unfathomable to the investigator, sometimes can mislead. To make certain I was on the right road, I wanted to run the experiment a second time, this time preferably with an active middle-aged woman. The patient with the proper specifications came into my office a few days later. She was fifty-six, had a big frame, weighed 190 pounds, and was experiencing tingling in her hands and an inability to completely flex her fingers. "Every time I sit down to watch television, my fingers start tingling and feel numb like they're asleep," she said.

"I've set up half the night lots of times, running warm water over my fingers trying to get some relief." She also had chest pain that seemed to spread into her arms and shoulders. A close look at her hands revealed puffy, swollen fingers. The woman was a perfect candidate for the B-complex study and was more than willing to participate—anything to get rid of the pain in her chest and fingers.

To rule out the possibility of other dietary factors having an effect, I asked the patient to step up her consumption of pork, eggs, butter, and gravies—animal fats—and we began the series of injections. Seven injections and two weeks later, we had a remarkably changed woman. "I can see the leaders in my hands better now," she said, and it was certainly true. I could see every tendon on the backs of her hands. The swelling that had previously concealed her tendons was gone. There was no edema. Although I had given but slight attention to the edema previously, I now realized, as the woman flexed her fingers perfectly, that the edema had prevented her from flexing them before. This struck me as highly significant. Furthermore, all of her other symptoms had improved. Her chest pain was gone, as was the pain in her shoulder, arms, and fingers. She hadn't had leg cramps for a week. And the tingling, my point of comparison, had disappeared.

This indicated that the woman and the dairyman both had been deficient in at least one of the five B vitamins I had treated them with. This also seemed to be true of the many others I had placed on the Morrison diet, pecans, and peanuts. The woman's case especially bothered me, however, for she was a cook in a school cafeteria and had been for eleven years, each day eating the same selection of food as the schoolchildren and teachers. My own four children ate every day at the same school cafeteria, a factor that deepened my emotional involvement. If my patient received an insufficient supply of the B vitamins from the school lunches, the same would be true of the children, a whole generation embarking on long-term vitamin-B deficiencies, sowing the seeds in childhood for future serious medical problems. And if this were happening in one school, might it not also be occurring in others? I thought it might be. I also suspected that it wasn't true of only school cafeterias, but of the American eating pattern in general.

A study of the symptoms sped up my process of determining which B-complex vitamin was responsible. I could eliminate three automatically. Vitamin-B$_1$ deficiency caused tremors of the tongue; B$_2$ deficiency, little raw cracks or sores in the corners of the mouth; and B$_3$ deficiency (the pellagra that Goldberger had fought), skin lesions of the hands and legs. My patients did not exhibit any of these three signs. Thus, I ruled out those vitamins. This left two poorly understood vitamins in the injections—B$_6$ and panthenol. Nobody had ever described a syndrome for B$_6$ deficiency in active adults. Therefore, I decided to inject vitamin-B$_6$ next. If that didn't work, I would test panthenol. If one of these last two nutrients worked to my satisfaction, I would thereafter use oral doses of the vitamin, a much preferable and less troublesome method for both physician and patient.

In order to keep the test conditions the same as with the previous patients, I needed to find a patient of about the same age, with the same symptoms and signs, and consuming the same high-fat diet. I ordered an injectable B$_6$ preparation, in the form of pyridoxine hydrochloride, and waited for a patient who was suffering from marked edema—the puffed, swollen condition I had found in the cafeteria cook. Edema was one of the knottiest problems facing medical science at the time. I was convinced, on the basis of my observation of the cook, that one of the remaining two B vitamins had cleared up her swollen hands. Had it been the B$_6$? I would soon know.

The first patient to receive the vitamin-B$_6$ injection alone was a thirty-seven-year-old woman who was eight months pregnant and weighed 195 pounds. This woman had severe tingling in both of her arms and hands, and swelling in her hands and feet. The tops of her feet were so swollen that her skin had a light sheen that was noticeable from across the room. When I pressed my finger into the top of her foot, the outline remained for several seconds.

"The swelling in my feet has been so bad I had to buy a size larger pair of house shoes," the woman said. "I couldn't get my regular shoes on, and my legs are sore to press on them. When I lie down at night I have cramps in the backs of my legs, between my knees and ankles. Every day after lunch when I get through ironing my clothes and doing my work, I lie down to rest a while. I no sooner get in bed than the tingling in my hands starts. I feel a numbness up to my elbow."

For my purposes, this woman was a perfect patient, but there were other factors that made me think very carefully about her case. It was May 26, 1962. This meant we were moving into the heat of a Texas summer, itself trial enough for anybody, much less a woman eight months pregnant. Swelling in the feet and ankles seemed to be more common during the summer months, and this woman had no air conditioning in her home. Furthermore, the woman was pregnant. Obstetricians had long entertained a theory that the pressure of the fetus on the veins of the mother's pelvis causes this type of swelling in the feet and legs. Most of them also believed that excessive consumption of table salt causes the swelling and for years had advised pregnant women to avoid eating salt. I agreed that Americans ate too much table salt, but now I wasn't sure this was the cause of edema of pregnancy. My patient also had symptoms other than swelling. Something else was at work. After consideration of the case and of the patient's individual needs, I went ahead with the B$_6$ injections, 50 milligrams every two days for a two-week period.

Four days later, when the pregnant woman returned for her third injection, what I saw made me hold my breath. I stared at her feet, the skin of which was now pliable, loose, and as wrinkled as if she had been swimming too long. It was an effort for the woman to keep her feet in the shoes that were now oversized. The numbness and tingling had left her hands, and the soreness in her legs had dramatically improved. Her right arm still had some residual tingling, but it was obvious that the symptoms were clearing up quickly. In four days, wrinkled, loose skin on normal sized hands and feet had replaced tight skin on puffy hands and feet. My patient had eaten a diet high in animal fats. There had been no mention of cutting back on salt. Edema, that big bugaboo of pregnancy, had been reduced by vitamin B$_6$ alone![3] It was the greatest thrill I have ever experienced in my medical career.

Chapter 11

YOUR COMPLETE NUTRITIONAL PROGRAM

Now that I have explained what vitamin B_6 is, how it works in the body, and how it helps against such disorders as coronary heart disease, diabetes, and carpal tunnel syndrome, it is time to turn our attention to the mechanics of taking B_6. The primary question is, "What is a safe daily dosage of vitamin B_6, and what is a toxic daily dosage?" Neurologist H. Schaumburg and his associates used electrical-conduction studies to determine that a daily dosage of 2,000 to 6,000 milligrams of vitamin B_6 could be toxic to the nerves in the dorsal root ganglia and to the peripheral sensory nerves in the feet and legs.[1]

In the Department of Neurology at Kaiser Permanente Medical Center in Hayward, California, neurologist Allan Bernstein, using electrical-conduction studies of the peripheral nerves, determined over a five-year period that patients with carpal tunnel syndrome and diabetic neuropathy who took 100 to 150 milligrams of vitamin B_6 daily displayed no electrical evidence of neurotoxicity.[2]

For thirty-three years, the citizens of Titus County, Texas (population 24,000), were encouraged by the news media and word of mouth to take vitamin B_6 as a daily supplement for the prevention of carpal tunnel syndrome, rheumatic diseases, the complications of diabetes, and degenerative diseases including atherosclerosis and acute myocardial infarction. In 1988, the monthly sales of 50- to 100-milligram tablets of vitamin B$_6$ totaled 59,200 tablets. In the first six months of 1994, according to an actual count of the invoices, the seven local pharmacies and one health food store sold an average of 61,400 tablets (614 bottles) of vitamin B$_6$ per month, which means that 2,046 tablets were taken daily by an estimated 1,500 people. During this seven-year period of brisk consumer consumption of vitamin B$_6$, the active Titus County Memorial Hospital medical staff of thirty-two physicians and surgeons neither saw nor examined a single patient with neurotoxicity caused by taking vitamin B$_6$. I have taken 50 to 200 milligrams of vitamin B$_6$ daily for thirty-five years. My four children, now healthy adults, were given 50 milligrams of vitamin B$_6$ daily beginning around the ages of eight to thirteen years. In addition, scientific articles prepared in collaboration with Dr. Karl Folkers and published over a seventeen-year period indicate that 50 to 300 milligrams is a safe daily dosage of vitamin B$_6$ for all adults including pregnant women, diabetics, and patients with coronary heart disease or carpal tunnel syndrome.

After my own thirty-five years of clinical research with vitamin B$_6$, my recommended therapeutic daily dosages, all proven safe, are as follows:

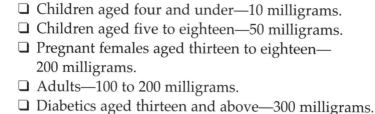

❏ Children aged four and under—10 milligrams.
❏ Children aged five to eighteen—50 milligrams.
❏ Pregnant females aged thirteen to eighteen—
    200 milligrams.
❏ Adults—100 to 200 milligrams.
❏ Diabetics aged thirteen and above—300 milligrams.

There are people who argue in support of the Recommended Dietary Allowance set by the National Research

Council of only 2 milligrams daily for healthy adults. Unfortunately, let me remind you that very few Americans eat a daily diet supplying even that much B_6. At the same time, I recommend caution against taking too much B_6. There may be mild but temporary sensory-nerve changes or toxicity when more than 1,000 milligrams of vitamin B_6 is taken daily.

Most processed foods have a good portion of their vitamins and minerals removed during the attempt to lengthen their shelf lives and keep them from spoiling. This is part of why obesity has become such a problem. Many people need to eat huge amounts of calories just to get the nutrients their bodies need and crave. And that familiar advice, "Don't eat so much, and exercise more," has been only partially successful. Jogging up and down the road helps some, but there is something about the brain and liver that is confused in relation to obesity. An obese individual may have a problem connected with brain function, taste, and hunger that must be corrected biochemically before any substantial amount of weight can be lost. Maintaining proper nutrition during the childhood and teen years may help to prevent obesity in adulthood.

A complete nutritional program should be implemented at the time of birth and continued throughout life. In fact, the best nutritional program is begun one month before conception. Women should take vitamin and mineral supplements including B_6 both during pregnancy and following birth if breastfeeding. The vitamins and minerals are passed from the mother to her baby through the breast milk. Babies of up to one year of age should be given vitamin drops on a daily basis. After the first birthday, children require calories for growth and energy. This means that children one year old need whole milk including the cream.

Physicians and scientists have studied the behavioral and mental development of infants and children born of young mothers suffering from malnutrition during pregnancy and have found that a certain characteristic appearance combined with functional abnormalities may be inborn. Down syndrome, caused by the presence of three rather than the normal two chromosomes designated as chromosome 21, is an example of this. It is not known whether the mental retardation of Down syndrome is the result of changes in the structure of the brain or of a potentially reversible chemical imbalance. It is known that if an expectant mother consumes alcohol or certain drugs, fetal abnormalities may result. Some scientists have also expressed concern about the intelligence and personality development of infants born of malnourished mothers. Nutritional supplements are often used in an effort to improve the emotional and mental capabilities of children of different ages.

Many of the multi-vitamin-and-mineral supplements on the market today contain some thirty important vitamins and minerals needed by the body for optimum health and longevity. If you don't like to swallow pills, you had better stay away from foods and drinks that are devoid of nutrients. Teach your children at an early age to eat a green salad every day as a part of their lunch. Give them fresh fruit and fruit juice for breakfast. Vitamins occur naturally in food and are needed for the metabolism of other nutrients. This is why nutritional supplements should be taken with meals if possible.

Foods that contain the B vitamins include red meat, especially liver, and fruit. Of all the fruits, bananas are the richest source of vitamin B_6. Pecans are also especially high in vitamin B_6. And don't forget the bountiful wheat hull. Spinach is rich in folic acid, and the chlorophyll in green plants has magnesium attached to it. Onions are a rich source of minerals in general. Natural foods contain vitamins and minerals that are far superior to those found in the many processed and fast-food products available. Life-preserving nutrients are necessary not only for enduring health and happiness, but for a sense of well-being.

Of course, bacteria—good and bad—are present in food, but they are also present in the body. With common sense, we can balance one against the other on the dinner table just like the human body does within the gastrointestinal system. Medical students sixty years ago were taught about salmonella and E. coli. Once in a while, an old hen will lay eggs that contain salmonella. Certain foods such as meat, chicken, eggs, and processed products like sausage and hamburger must be cooked in order to kill pathogenic (disease-causing) bacteria. The food industry knows and understands this just as you and I do. But there is an associated tragedy—the necessary cooking and processing undertaken by the food industry and the family cook destroys the B vitamins. In a beef roast cooked at 400°F (Fahrenheit), about 40 percent of the vitamin B_6 is destroyed. In like manner, the folic acid is destroyed. At best, processed and cooked foods have a reduced nutrient content. The alternative at this point is the use of vitamin and mineral supplements.

Consider a thirty-nine-year-old woman who came to me complaining of a tingling numbness in her fingers and hands. She could not bend her right index finger toward her thumb with enough strength to hold a pencil. One year later, after she had followed a daily regimen including 50 milligrams of vitamin B_6, her hands were pain-free. Her hands remained pain-free until she moved to Israel due her husband's job transfer. By the end of the first month, she had used up her vitamin-B_6 tablets, but since she was doing well, she did not bother to replace them. Furthermore, even though she didn't know it, she was probably getting a good "average" amount of vitamin B_6 from her diet. She and her husband lived in a farming community about twelve miles from Tel Aviv. They ate lots of fresh fruits and vegetables. Eggplants and potatoes were their primary vegetables, and oranges, apples, grapes, and dates were their primary fruits. Although meat was rare, they also had cheese, frozen fish, eggs, and some chicken. Presumably, if this woman had had a "normal" need for B_6, her diet would have supplied it. But remember, about 2 or 3 milligrams a day is about all the B_6 we get from food, and it is nearly impossible to get more than 5 milligrams a day.

About six weeks after she took her last B$_6$ tablet, the woman found her symptoms recurring. It was a crisis in her life and, therefore, in the life of her husband, too, especially since they were unable to find vitamin-B$_6$ tablets anywhere in Tel Aviv. "My husband told the Israeli officials to get me some vitamin B$_6$ tablets," she said. Finally, after about three months, the Israelis finished making the necessary arrangements with customs, and B$_6$ tablets were delivered to the woman's front door.

The woman was at menopausal age, but when I saw her again seven years later, she had been taking 50 milligrams of B$_6$ daily and was still menstruating regularly. Her case showed that the disorder among women labeled "menopausal arthritis" isn't always menopausal. And the woman learned over those seven years that, at least as far as she was concerned, 100 milligrams of B$_6$ daily controls premenstrual edema better than 50 milligrams does.

Vitamin-B$_6$ deficiency is capable of distorting fluid balance, mineral balance, and hormonal balance. Great numbers of Americans are walking around with five to seven pounds of excess fluid in their bodies that could be eliminated by taking B$_6$. If B$_6$ is not diuretic in the usual sense, then it has a striking effect on intracellular biochemical exchanges, the exact nature of which is yet to be revealed. But the fact that associated neuropathies are improved as edema subsides indicates that vitamin B$_6$ has more than a simple diuretic effect.

Of utmost importance is the fact that "coronary prone" individuals have similar symptoms, including edema, numbness and tingling, and disturbance of the hand grip. One has only to know that rheumatism and shoulder-hand syndrome are responsive to vitamin B$_6$ to conclude that, somewhere between the early life of the fetus and the terminal gasps of the coronary-thrombosis victim, an increased need for vitamin B$_6$ stands paramount as an associate in the cause of the deadly heart attack.

In this book, I have described a large number of cases that attest to the medicinal values of vitamin B_6. I have also presented supportive evidence from the laboratory to back up my clinical findings. When there is objective evidence of clinical improvement of signs and symptoms in humans, it transcends anything seen anywhere else. It is proof positive. And when laboratory and clinical data form a dovetail, there can be no doubt.

Chapter 12

YOU AND YOUR DOCTOR

There is something personal about the care of a doctor for a patient—a confidence and respect shared one for the other. In the presence of fear, anxiety, pain, and loss of strength on the part of the patient, a degree of trust must also exist. This is true regardless of whether the doctor practices in a crossroads western town or at a huge hospital in a great city. The doctor-patient relationship is almost sacred.

The most important thing to a doctor is that his or her patients be given the best, most up-to-date medical attention for their symptoms. When a substance or medication works for a specific disorder, doctors want to use it for that disorder. However, there is a large gap between the clinic and the laboratory regarding techniques. In the laboratory, researchers can demand precision in techniques, as well as in results, because they work with experimental animals. But in the clinic, precision is not possible because doctors care for human beings. Many diagnoses are, by necessity, educated guesses, since even diagnostic tests are not always definitive. Moreover, a doctor cannot always be sure which test is the best to give a patient. In the clinic, the human factor is forever present. Observation and judgment are required. And when making a diagnosis and prescribing treatment, doctors are most likely to find these tools to also be the most effective in fighting disease.

Dr. Jan Bonsma of the University of Praetoria, South Africa, taught a year at Texas A. and M. University a while ago. He was an authority on animal husbandry and could accurately determine the fertility of a cow using only visual examination. He had a trained eye and knew what to look for. After practicing his skills in my cow pasture, he told me, "It is the observation of the slight deviation from the normal that makes a good doctor. If one observes more thoroughly than the other, then he is the better doctor."

The same can be said for patients. Patients, too, must be observant, noting changes in their bodies that, whether or not related to disease conditions, might be of interest to a doctor who is trying to determine cause and effect. Food cravings are significant in relation to nutritional deficiencies and are one way the body has for alerting us that its fine-tuned workings are off balance. Your body will talk to you if you listen carefully.

Nutrition has a special relevance for today's patients, particularly when you remember that by the time wheat is milled and white bread is marketed, about 95 percent of its original B_6 content has been removed or destroyed. Glutamate from bread is necessary for brain energy, and glutamate requires the assistance of vitamin B_6 to be metabolized in the brain. Put simply, food that is taken into the stomach becomes, within two hours, a liquid mixture of chemicals that must quickly be changed, with the assistance of other substances, into the metabolites needed by the cells in the different organs. If not changed quickly enough or completely, some of these metabolites become toxic. If sufficient vitamin B_6 were reintroduced into commonly used food products such as bread and milk, the present nationwide B_6 deficiency would eventually be eliminated, leading to the eradication of many of today's common disorders.

It has always been the practice of doctors to do the best with what they have. Fortunately, the horse-and-buggy days are gone. The roads are better, and medical and surgical equipment is vastly improved. Millions and billions of dollars flow through today's health industry. But two disease conditions have thrown the medical profession into a state of paradox—coronary heart disease, the leading killer disease in the United States, and diabetes, the most costly disease in the United States. Prevention of these conditions has become paramount and must be practiced from the cradle to old age. Included in prevention are proper nutrition and lifestyle.

Doctors cannot do it all. The food industry must improve the ways food is processed and marketed. Dietitians and nurses must be trained to advise sick patients about diet. The public must be educated about proper nutrition. This is a good opportunity for everyone to practice cooperation to the full extent of the word's definition. From the food industry to the media, from the scientific community to patients, everyone must pitch in and work for improved preventive care. This change will not happen overnight, however. The quick fixes of the post–World War II era, including penicillin, long ago jaded the public's imagination. The results offered by vitamins seem to take such a long time to materialize, especially next to quick-acting medications, and the information that is currently available on vitamins is so massive that we become worn out just trying to determine what we actually need.

In truth, however, taking nutritional supplements is the only wide-scale answer. Let the arguments over dosage come forth. I have written my opinion. The next doctor may have another opinion. You should discuss the dosage that is proper for you with the doctor you most admire and trust with your life.

I cannot recommend a doctor for you, nor can I prescribe a regimen of daily nutritional supplements that is perfect for your particular needs. We must each take the responsibility for educating ourselves about our own bodies. A look at the practices of animal husbandry will quickly reaffirm the fact that we often take better care of our animals then we do ourselves. A doctor can diagnose a disease, even test for nutritional deficiencies, but it is the patient's desire to take care of him- or herself by using all available medicines and medical procedures that determines the outcome. Since you are reading this book, you are on the road to better health and a more confident relationship with a doctor who has taken an oath to help keep you on the right track.

CONCLUSION

On December 18, 1942, I was awarded my Medical Doctor degree at a graduation ceremony in Galveston, Texas. I was also presented with a beautifully decorated copy of the Oath of Hippocrates, as were all the graduates, but was never asked to swear the Oath. I was not even asked to read the statement or save it. But, this ethical direction from ancient Greece, written around 400 B.C., still guides me, as it does my fellow graduates and all physicians who spend their professional lives taking care of sick people. Priceless information on vitamin B_6 comes from physicians and scientists around the world who strive to uphold the Oath by solving medical mysteries and bringing new hope for tomorrow.

At the turn of the twentieth century, hospitals were built, financed, and managed as parts of highly respected church or religious organizations. Physicians and surgeons felt honored to staff these medical facilities. Later, the Veterans' Administration opened hospitals for the men and women who served our nation in war and peacetime, and large cities opened hospitals for the indigent. Today, medical care has been extended to cover numerous disease conditions, as well as the aged, the blind, the homebound, and the insane. The cost to the federal and state governments has increased to billions of dollars. But—and this is one of the most important questions that has ever been asked—who is focusing on the prevention of disease?

Vitamin B$_6$ is an excellent tool for the prevention of a variety of diseases plaguing our modern civilization. However, people need to be educated and guided in its use. For example, the dosing amount and frequency used by a fifty-year-old woman to prevent or treat carpal tunnel syndrome are different from what should be given to a five-year-old child to prevent coronary heart disease in later life. These are further different from what should be used by a pregnant woman to prevent a B$_6$ deficiency in her unborn child, and different again from what should be used by a diabetic. Who is educating these people—the "masses"—about vitamin-B$_6$ therapy, as well as other forms of preventive healthcare? The drug companies aren't doing it. Many doctors aren't doing it. And even the government, which has the most to gain considering the huge annual expenditures involving Medicare and Medicaid, isn't doing it.

Why is vitamin B$_6$ so wonderful as a preventive-healthcare therapy? Because of its functions in the body. Once B$_6$ is taken into the body, it is transformed into pyridoxal phosphate. Pyridoxal phosphate is a coenzyme—that is, a substance that functions to activate (set into motion) enzymes and enzyme systems. Enzymes trigger virtually every activity within our bodies. Without sufficient pyridoxal phosphate present to activate them, important enzymes cannot function. Chief among the biochemical actions sparked by vitamin B$_6$ are those that control the metabolism of protein.

After you swallow a bite of steak, digestive secretions break the protein in the steak into amino acids. For the amino acids to be absorbed through the intestinal wall, however, pyridoxal phosphate must be present in the body. To add to matters, besides needing B$_6$ to activate the enzymes necessary for their absorption, amino acids also need B_6 as part of their composition. Furthermore, vitamin B_6 itself requires the assistance of an enzyme that contains amino acids in order to function. This means that a deficiency of B_6 can actually feed upon itself. Amino acids are often referred to as the "building blocks" of living organisms. Our physical bodies need amino acids to survive. Even some vitamins need amino acids to function, which means they also need B_6. While the process of aging has not yet been clearly defined biochemically, it certainly involves the functional failure of amino acids and the multitude of enzymes that contain them.[1]

After thirty-five years of clinical research with vitamin B_6, I have come up with safe and effective daily-dosage recommendations for all the age groups, pregnant women, and diabetics. These were presented in Chapter 11. There are people who feel these recommendations are too high, who argue in support of the RDAs set by the National Research Council, which include roughly 2 milligrams per day for healthy adults. Unfortunately, my studies, as well as studies conducted by other researchers, have shown that 2 milligrams is not nearly enough to either prevent or treat coronary heart disease, diabetes, and a number of the other disorders that are ravaging our modern society.

There are also people who argue that nutritional supplements are unnecessary. Since few Americans eat a daily diet supplying even the RDA of B_6, supplements are a necessity today. Trace-nutrient authority Dr. Henry A. Schroeder reviewed the laboratory data on hundreds of processed food products analyzed for B_6 content and found that, for example, vegetables lost from 57 to 77 percent of their original B_6 content during the canning process. Frozen vegetables showed losses of 37 to 77 percent. Frozen fruit juices, canned meats, and some processed meats all lost B_6, too. About 80 percent of the original B_6 disappeared when wheat was made into all-purpose flour. Precooked rice showed losses of 93 percent of its original B_6 content.[2] Naturally, consuming a diet of fresh raw fruits (especially bananas, which gram for gram are about five times richer in B_6 content than any other fruit) and vegetables boosts B_6 intake. Walnuts, filberts, peanuts, and sunflower seeds also are rich in B_6, as are liver, lean muscle meats, white chicken-breast meat, and fish, as well as wheat germ, soybean flour, and sunflower-seed flour. But, if disease conditions already exist in a body, it is highly unlikely that even an all-natural diet will ever supply all the B_6 that is necessary.

Some scientists contend that certain blood data do not show consistent B_6 deficiency as determined in the laboratory. My response is that a number of urine and blood-plasma levels are capable of changing, going up or down, within a twenty-four-hour period. These test results do not correlate with the definite clinical improvements displayed by patients following therapy with vitamin B_6 for ninety days. At the end of three months of therapy, more accurate evaluations can be made by the patients themselves, plus their physicians, surgeons, and other caregivers. A patient may have two disease conditions, even two types of the same disease condition, at the same time. An evaluation made after three months of treatment will separate these conditions regarding vitamin B_6 and continued therapy. In no way is this to be taken as a criticism of associated laboratory data. Biochemists have done marvelous research with vitamin B_6. Objective clinical evidence, however, must be given precedence over laboratory data that can change in one day. It takes the correlation of objective clinical improvements over a ninety-day period with precise biochemical data to determine the existence of a severe vitamin-B_6 deficiency.

More than 225 scientific articles have been published presenting proof that homocysteine contributes to calcification and blockage in the arteries. Cardiologists from the Cleveland Clinic, in a symposium in Florida in 1996 and again in California in 1997, presented evidence that high homocysteine and low vitamin-B_6 levels are independent risk factors for coronary heart disease. Kilmer McCully and I completed an epidemiological study in 1995 that showed the importance of vitamin B_6 in relation to, among other things, coronary heart disease. What more can I say about how vital vitamin B_6 is in the fight against the leading killer disease in the United States?

The government's current dietary guidelines for Americans include recommendations for persons aged two years old through adulthood, and, according to Eileen Kennedy, D.Sc., director of the Center for Nutrition Policy and Promotion of the Department of Agriculture, the revision due in the year 2000 *may* include guidelines for children below two. "The issue is not whether guidelines for children need to be developed, but how best to promote the information that exists," says Ms. Kennedy.[3] My hope is that concerned officials will take note of children's needs for vitamin B_6.

I mailed letters voicing my feelings on the importance of fortifying food with B_6 to President Bill Clinton and FDA commissioner Dr. David Kessler. In February 1994, I received a reply from Joanne N. Hough, policy analyst, FDA Executive Secretariat, noting that the FDA is aware of the research concerning vitamin B_6. "However, there is no widely accepted scientific evidence that these diseases are the result of *dietary* deficiency of vitamin B_6," Ms. Hough said. "Neither the RDAs [Recommended Dietary Allowances], the USRDAs [U.S. Recommended Daily Allowances], nor RDIs [Reference Daily Intakes] are intended to apply to people with nutritional needs that are unusual due to disease, surgery, or metabolic disorders." However, despite its refusal to consider B_6 fortification at this time, the FDA did publish a proposal in the Federal Register on October 8, 1993, to add folic acid to flour, bread, and other grain products to lower the risk of neural tube defects in babies.[4] Further exposure must be given to the scientific studies on the benefits of vitamin B_6 in order to help unite the experts' opinions about this nutrient, stop the questioning about its importance, and encourage the FDA to recognize its connection to health.

Having spent over thirty years conducting research on vitamin B$_6$ and having proven that extensive vitamin-B$_6$ deficiency exists in eastern Texas, I fear the federal government is facing a national tragedy. No one physician, or group of physicians, can put vitamin B$_6$ into the stomachs of all American citizens to prevent the disease conditions caused by deficiency of the nutrient. I have traveled to Washington, D.C. four times in the last several years in an effort to improve federal policy regarding vitamin B$_6$. I was informed that, by law, I had the right to present a Citizen Petition. I completed such a petition, urging the "fortification of foods with vitamin B$_6$," and presented it to the Department of Health and Human Services of the Food and Drug Administration in 1995. The petition was assigned docket number 95P-0392/CP1, and I encourage interested persons to contribute pertinent information.

In a letter of support contained within my petition, Bill Francis, executive director of Natural Food Associates, notes, "Replicated analyses have confirmed nutritional decreases and inadequacies in virtually 100 percent of the food samples reviewed for the last forty years; foods subject to over-processing and adulteration are further compromised, in terms of their nutritional integrity. Virtually on a daily basis this vitamin [B$_6$] is further qualified as an essential nutrient of extreme importance."[5] In another letter of support, David Ponsonby, M.Ed., a health educator, notes that while the organic whole-food diet from the years before World War II had sufficient B$_6$ content, "today, although we have a label on flour which states 'enriched,' the level of enrichment is still only some 14 percent of the pre-processing whole grain level. The new food pyramid has breads and cereals as its foundation. How good a structure can this be in light of these statistics? People eat one-quarter of the recommended servings of grains per day, each serving of which, even if eaten, still represents only 14 percent the nutrition enjoyed under 'natural' conditions."[6]

Though the FDA stands by its recommended 2.0-milligram-per-day quota of vitamin B_6, you should be aware that you need to consume six slices of whole-wheat bread to get just .312 milligram of vitamin B_6, one cup of whole cow's milk to get just .102 milligram, one pound of broiled lean beef to get just .836 milligram, and one pound of bananas to get a whopping 2.622 milligrams. This data is from a computer in the Clinical Nutrition Section of Titus Regional Medical Center and is intended just to show how much food needs to be consumed on a daily basis to obtain even the RDA of vitamin B_6.[7]

A person of any age can safely consume 10 milligrams of vitamin B_6 daily. This should be the goal of any nutritional-supplement program. The Department of Health and Human Services must take the lead and encourage Americans to strive for this goal. It is my firm conviction that in addition to encouraging individuals to take vitamin-B_6 supplements, the Department of Health and Human Services should also encourage the addition of 3 milligrams of vitamin B_6 to every six ounces of pasteurized cow's milk, every half-pound of bread, and every pound of processed meat.

The data concluding that 2,000 milligrams of vitamin B_6 taken daily is toxic cannot be ignored. Determining correct vitamin dosages is an extremely complex undertaking. It is possible for the average physical laborer to eat enough natural foods to get about 10.0 milligrams of vitamin B_6 daily. At the same time, however, the average pregnant woman might eat a diet supplying as little as 2.5 milligrams of vitamin B_6 daily and still safely deliver a normal baby. Dosages of vitamin B_6 greater than 300 milligrams per day are not recommended in the treatment of general disease conditions. However, the successful treatment and prevention of disease conditions caused by serious vitamin-B_6 deficiency may necessitate the use of 300 milligrams daily. This dosage has been proven safe for both expectant mothers and their developing babies. In fact, vitamin B_6 taken at a dosage of 200 milligrams per day should be a part of every woman's prenatal care.

Great numbers of young women begin pregnancy eating less than 2.0 milligrams of vitamin B$_6$ daily. Even more tragic, millions of American children will enter the twenty-first century consuming a diet that provides less than 1.5 milligrams of vitamin B$_6$ daily. A consumer-driven demand for preventive healthcare comes from the understanding that vitamins are to enzymes like sunshine is to roses. There is wisdom in accepting preventive medicine as an integral part of the healing arts. So much information has been assembled by thousands of physicians, surgeons, and scientists. The time has arrived for the government and the food industry to throw their hats into the arena and join the effort to rescue the human race.

NOTES

Introduction

1. Milton Kochler, "B$_6$—The Vitamin That Vanishes With Youth," *Prevention*, March 1973, pp. 79–84.

2. E.R. Monsen, "The 10th Edition of the Recommended Dietary Allowances (RDAs) 1989," *Journal of the American Dietetic Association* 89 (December 1989), pp. 1748–1752.

3. J.Y. Lu, D.L. Cook, J.B. Jarvis, Z.A. Kirmani, C.C. Liu, D.N. Makadia, T.A. Makadam, O.B. Omasayie, D.P. Patel, V.J. Reddy, B.W. Walker, C.S. Williams, and R.A. Chung, "Intakes of Vitamins and Minerals by Pregnant Women With Selected Clinical Symptoms," *Journal of the American Diabetic Association* 78 (May 1981), pp. 477–481.

4. John M. Ellis and James Presley, *Vitamin B$_6$: The Doctor's Report* (New York: Harper and Row, 1973), pp. 97–113.

5. J.M. Ellis, "Treatment of Carpal Tunnel Syndrome With Vitamin B$_6$," *Southern Medical Journal* 80 (July 1987), pp. 882–884.

6. D.C. Shepard, J.B. Hitz, and J.A. Dain, "Pyridoxal-5-Phosphate Inhibits Nonenzymatic Glycosylation of Proteins," *Biochemical Archives* 1 (1985), pp. 143–151.

7. L.R. Solomon and K. Cohen, "Erythrocyte 02 Transport and Metabolism and Effects of Vitamin B₆ Therapy in Type II Diabetes Mellitus," *Diabetes* 38 (July 1989), pp. 881–886.

8. M. Khatami, "Role of Pyridoxal Phosphate/Pyridoxine in Diabetes," *Annals of the New York Academy of Sciences* 585 (1990), pp 502–504.

9. John M. Ellis, Karl Folkers, Michael Minadeo, Ronald Van Buskirk, Li-Jun Xia, and Hiroo Tamagawa, "A Deficiency of Vitamin B₆ Is a Plausible Molecular Basis of the Retinopathy of Patients With Diabetes Mellitus," *Biochemical and Biophysical Research Communications* 179 (30 August 1991), pp. 615–619.

10. John Marion Ellis, *Diabetes New Therapies: Clinically Proven Usage of Vitamin B₆* (Waco, Texas; Texian Press, 1995), pp. 43–134.

11. J.M. Ellis, *The Doctor Who Looked at Hands* (New York: Vantage Press, 1966), pp. 231–235.

12. K.S. McCully, "Chemical Pathology of Homocysteine," part 1: "Atherogenesis," *Annals of Clinical and Laboratory Science* 23 (1993), pp. 477–493.

13. John M. Ellis and Kilmer S. McCully, "Prevention of Myocardial Infarction by Vitamin B₆," *Research Communications in Molecular Pathology and Pharmacology* 89 (August 1995), pp. 208–220.

14. John M. Ellis, *Free of Pain: The Cause of Soft Tissue Rheumatism*, revised edition update (Dallas: Southwest Publishing Co., 1983), pp. 3–6.

15. Ellis and Presley, pp. 205–206.

16. R.R. Brown, "Normal and Pathological Conditions Which May Alter the Human Requirement for Vitamin B$_6$," *Journal of Agriculture and Food Chemistry*, n.d.

17. Esmond E. Snell, "Summary of Session I and Some Notes on the Metabolism of Vitamin B$_6$," *Vitamins and Hormones* 22 (1964), pp. 485–494.

18. Paul György, "Developments Leading to the Metabolic Role of Vitamin B$_6$," *American Journal of Clinical Nutrition* 24 (October 1971), pp. 1250–1256.

Chapter 1
The Importance of Vitamin B$_6$

1. E.R. Monsen, "The 10th Edition of the Recommended Dietary Allowances (RDAs) 1989," *Journal of the American Dietetic Association* 89 (December 1989), pp. 1748–1752.

2. J.D. Ribaya-Mercado, et al., "Vitamin B$_6$ Requirement of Elderly Men and Women," *Journal of Nutrition* 121 (1991), pp. 1062–1074.

3. John Marion Ellis, *Diabetes New Therapies: Clinically Proven Usage of Vitamin B$_6$* (Waco, Texas: Texian Press, 1995), p. 30.

4. Judy Shabert and Nancy Ehrlich, *The Ultimate Nutrient Glutamine: The Essential Nonessential Amino Acid* (Garden City Park, New York: Avery Publishing Group, 1994), p. 87.

5. John M. Ellis and Kilmer S. McCully, "Prevention of Myocardial Infarction by Vitamin B$_6$," *Research Communications in Molecular Pathology and Pharmacology* 89 (August 1995), pp. 208–220.

6. Ellis, pp. 30–32.

7. C.H. Hill and Chun Su Kim, "The Derangement of Elastin Synthesis in Pyridoxine Deficiency," *Biochemical and Biophysical Research Communications* 27 (1997), pp. 94–99.

8. J.C. Murray, D.R. Fraser, and C.I. Levene, "The Effect of Pyridoxine Deficiency on Lysyl Oxidase Activity in the Chick," *Experimental and Molecular Pathology* 28 (1978), pp. 301–308.

9. P.G. Masse, F. Gerber, V.E. Colombo, and H. Weiser, "Ultrastructural Defects in the Cartilage Collagen Caused by Vitamin B$_6$ Deficiency," *Annals of the New York Academy of Sciences* 585 (1990), pp. 522–525.

10. D.C. Shepard, J.B. Hitz, and J.A. Dain, "Pyridoxal-5-Phosphate Inhibits Nonenzymatic Glycosylation of Proteins," *Biochemical Archives* 1 (1985), pp. 143–151.

11. L.R. Solomon and K. Cohen, "Erythrocyte 02 Transport and Metabolism and Effects of Vitamin B$_6$ Therapy in Type II Diabetes Mellitus," *Diabetes* 38 (July 1989), pp. 881–886.

12. M. Khatami, "Role of Pyridoxal Phosphate/Pyridoxine in Diabetes," *Annals of the New York Academy of Sciences* 585 (1990), pp 502–504.

13. Ellis and McCully, pp. 208–220.

14. K.S. McCully, "Vascular Pathology of Homocysteinemia: Implications for the Pathogenesis of Arteriosclerosis," *American Journal of Pathology* 66 (1969), pp. 111–128.

15. K.S. McCully, "Homocysteine Theory of Arteriosclerosis: Development and Current Status," in A.M. Gotto Jr. and R. Paoletti, editors, *Atherosclerosis Reviews*, volume 11 (New York: Raven Press, 1983), pp. 157–246.

16. K.S. McCully, "Chemical Pathology of Homocysteine," part 1: "Atherogenesis," *Annals of Clinical and Laboratory Science* 23 (1993), pp. 477–493.

17. "Homocysteine Theory of Arteriosclerosis: Development and Current Status," pp. 157–246.

18. S.H. Mudd, F. Skovby, H.L. Levy, K.D. Pettigrew, B. Wilcken, R.E. Pyeritz, G. Andria, G.H.J. Boers, I.L. Bromberg, R. Cerone, B. Fowler, H. Grobe, H. Schmidt, and L. Schweitzer, "The Natural History of Homocystinuria Due to Cystathionine Beta Synthase Deficiency," *American Journal of Human Genetics* 37 (1985), pp. 1–31.

19. M.M. Suzman, "Effect of Pyridoxine and Low Animal Protein Diet in Coronary Heart Disease," *Circulation* 48 (1973), supplement IV, p. 254.

20. Ellis, pp. 32–34.

Chapter 2
How Vitamin B$_6$ Works

1. John M. Ellis, Karl Folkers, Michael Minadeo, Ronald Van Buskirk, Li-Jun Xia, and Hiroo Tamagawa, "A Deficiency of Vitamin B$_6$ Is a Plausible Molecular Basis of the Retinopathy of Patients With Diabetes Mellitus," *Biochemical and Biophysical Research Communications* 179 (30 August 1991), pp. 615–619.

2. K.S. Rogers, E.S. Higgins, and E.S. Kline, "Experimental Diabetes Causes Mitochondrial Loss and Cytoplasmic Enrichment of Pyridoxal Phosphate and Aspartate Aminotransferase Activity," *Biochemical Medicine and Metabolic Biology* 36 (1986), pp. 91–97.

3. G.S. Phalen, "Reflections on 21 Years Experience With

the Carpal Tunnel Syndrome," *Journal of the American Medical Association* 212 (1970), pp. 1365–1367.

4. Ellis, Folkers, Minadeo, Van Buskirk, Xia, and Tamagawa, pp. 615–619.

5. J.M. Ellis, "Treatment of Carpal Tunnel Syndrome With Vitamin B$_6$," *Southern Medical Journal* 80 (July 1987), pp. 882–884.

6. J.M. Ellis and K. Folkers, "Clinical Aspects of Treatment of Carpal Tunnel Syndrome With Vitamin B$_6$," *Annals of the New York Academy of Sciences* 585 (1990), pp. 302–320.

7. Ellis, Folkers, Minadeo, Van Buskirk, Xia, and Tamagawa, pp. 615–619.

8. Mitchel L. Zoler, "Folic Acid Cuts Homocysteine Levels in CV Disease," *Family Practice News*, 15 January 1997, pp. 20a–20b.

9. B. Rimland, E. Callaway, and P. Dreyfus, "The Effects of High Doses of Vitamin B$_6$ on Autistic Children: A Double-Blind Study," *American Journal of Psychiatry* 135 (1978), pp. 472–475.

10. B. Rimland, "Controversies in the Treatment of Autistic Children: Vitamin and Drug Therapy," *Journal of Child Neurology* 3 (1988), supplement, pp. 568–572.

11. A. Sjogren, C.-H. Floren, and A. Nilsson, "Magnesium Deficiency in IDDM Related to Level of Glycosylated Hemoglobin," *Diabetes* 35 (1986), pp. 459–463.

12. P. McNair, C. Christiansen, C. Madsbad, et al., "Hypomagnesemia: A Risk Factor in Diabetic Retinopathy," *Diabetes* 27 (1978), pp. 1075–1077.

13. H.M. Mather, G.E. Levin, and J.A. Nisbet, "Hypomagnesemia and Symptomatic Ischemic Heart Disease in Diabetes," *Magnesium Bulletin* 3 (1981), pp. 169–172.

14. G.W. Evans, "Effect of Chromium Picolinate on Insulin Controlled Parameters in Humans," *International Journal of Biosocial and Medical Research* 11 (1989), pp. 163–180.

15. G.W. Evans, "An Inexpensive, Convenient Adjunct for the Treatment of Diabetes," *Western Journal of Medicine* 155 (1991), p. 549.

16. John M. Ellis and James Presley, *Vitamin B$_6$: The Doctor's Report* (New York: Harper and Row, 1973), pp. xiii–xv.

17. A.E. Braunstein, "Pyridoxal Phosphate," in P.D. Boyer, H.A. Lardy, and K. Myrback, editors, *The Enzymes*, volume 2 (New York: Academic Press, 1960), pp. 113–184.

Chapter 3
The History of Vitamin B$_6$

1. John M. Ellis and James Presley, *Vitamin B$_6$: The Doctor's Report* (New York: Harper and Row, 1973), pp. 12–38.

2. Paul György, "Developments Leading to the Metabolic Role of Vitamin B$_6$," *American Journal of Clinical Nutrition* 24 (October 1971), pp. 1250–1256.

3. Paul György, "The History of Vitamin B$_6$: Introductory Remarks," *Vitamins and Hormones* 22 (1964), pp. 361–365.

4. Tom D. Spies, William B. Bean, and William F. Ashe, "A Note on the Use of Vitamin B$_6$ in Human Nutrition," *Journal of the American Medical Association* (10 June 1939), pp. 2414–2415. See also "24-Hour Recoveries Result From Synthesized Vitamin," *Science News Letter*, 24 June 1939, p. 395.

5. Ellis and Presley, pp. 12–38. See also *Science News Letter* (1 June 1940), p. 340.

6. Samuel Lepkovsky, Elisabeth Roboz, and A.J. Haagen-Smit, "Xanthurenic Acid and Its Role in the Tryptophan

Metabolism of Pyridoxine-Deficient Rats," *Journal of Biological Chemistry* 149 (1943), pp. 195–201.

7. Max Wachstein, "Evidence for a Relative Vitamin B$_6$ Deficiency in Pregnancy and Some Disease States," *Vitamins and Hormones* 22 (1964), pp. 705–719.

8. "Developments Leading to the Metabolic Role of Vitamin B$_6$," pp. 1250–1256.

9. Howard Glassford, "Report," *Today's Health* (December 1954), pp. 26–27, 44. Also see "Vitamin B$_6$ in Human Nutrition," in *Report of the Tenth M & R Pediatric Research Conference* (Columbus, Ohio: M & R Laboratories, 1954), p. 59.

10. Richard W. Vilter, "The Vitamin B$_6$–Hydrazide Relationship," *Vitamins and Hormones* 22 (1964), pp. 797–805.

11. John W. Harris and Daniel L. Horrigan, "Pyridoxine-Responsive Anemia: Prototype and Variations on the Theme," *Vitamins and Hormones* 22 (1964), pp. 721–753.

12. "Developments Leading to the Metabolic Role of Vitamin B$_6$," pp. 1250–1256.

13. Ellis and Presley, pp. 12–38. See also "Serendipitous Sulphonylureas," *Journal of the American Medical Association* 219 (6 March 1972), p. 1335.

14. Paul Paris, "Treating Diabetes With B$_6$," *Longview News-Journal*, 19 October 1995, pp. 1D–2D.

15. J.F. Rinehart and L.D. Greenberg, "Pathogenesis of Experimental Arteriosclerosis in Pyridoxine Deficiency: With Notes on Similarities to Human Arteriosclerosis," *Archives of Pathology* 51 (1951), pp. 12–18.

16. K.S. McCully, "Chemical Pathology of Homocysteine," part 1: "Atherogenesis," *Annals of Clinical and Laboratory Science* 23 (1993), pp. 477–493.

17. K. Folkers, J. Ellis, T. Watanabe, S. Saji, and M. Kaji, "Biochemical Evidence for a Deficiency of Vitamin B$_6$ in the Carpal Tunnel Syndrome Based on a Cross-Over Clinical Study," *Proceedings of the National Academy of Sciences* (1978), pp. 3410–3412.

18. J.M. Ellis and K. Folkers, "Clinical Aspects of Treatment of Carpal Tunnel Syndrome With Vitamin B$_6$," *Annals of the New York Academy of Sciences* 585 (1990), pp. 302–320.

19. J.M. Ellis, "Treatment of Carpal Tunnel Syndrome With Vitamin B$_6$," *Southern Medical Journal* 80 (July 1987), pp. 882–884.

20. M. Stamfer, M. Malinow, W. Willett, L. Newcomer, B. Upson, D. Ullmann, P. Tishler, and C. Hennekens, "A Prospective Study of Plasma Homocysteine and Risk of Myocardial Infarction in U.S. Physicians," *Journal of the American Medical Association* 270 (1992), pp. 2693–2698.

21. K. Robinson, E. Mayer, M. Miller, R. Green, F. Lente, A. Gupta, K. Kottke-Marchant, S. Savon, J. Selub, S. Nissen, M. Kutner, E. Topol, and D. Jacobson, "Hyper-homocysteinemia and Low Pyridoxal Phosphate Common and Independent Reversible Risk Factors for Coronary Artery Disease," *Circulation* 92 (15 November 1995), pp. 2825–2830.

22. John M. Ellis, Karl Folkers, Michael Minadeo, Ronald Van Buskirk, Li-Jun Xia, and Hiroo Tamagawa, "A Deficiency of Vitamin B$_6$ Is a Plausible Molecular Basis of the Retinopathy of Patients With Diabetes Mellitus," *Biochemical and Biophysical Research Communications* 179 (30 August 1991), pp. 615–619.

23. K. Rogers and C. Mohan, "Mini-Review Vitamin B$_6$ Metabolism and Diabetes," *Biochemical Medicine and Metabolic Biology* 52 (1994), pp. 10–17.

24. John M. Ellis and Kilmer S. McCully, "Prevention of Myocardial Infarction by Vitamin B$_6$," *Research Communications in Molecular Pathology and Pharmacology* 89 (August 1995), pp. 208–220.

Chapter 4
Carpal Tunnel Syndrome

1. Ralph Ware, "Carpal Tunnel Syndrome," *Natural Food and Farming*, January-February 1993, pp. 7–9.

2. Ann Meyer, "Carpal Tunnel Syndrome: Surprise—You May Be At Risk," *Better Homes and Gardens*, June 1991, pp. 38, 40.

3. Cal Orey, "Preventing Carpal Tunnel Syndrome," *Fitness Plus—Better Health for Every Body*, March 1991, pp. 66, 124.

4. K. Folkers, J. Ellis, T. Watanabe, S. Saji, and M. Kaji, "Biochemical Evidence for a Deficiency of Vitamin B$_6$ in the Carpal Tunnel Syndrome Based on a Cross-Over Clinical Study," *Proceedings of the National Academy of Sciences* (1978), pp. 3410–3412.

5. J.M. Ellis and K. Folkers, "Clinical Aspects of Treatment of Carpal Tunnel Syndrome With Vitamin B$_6$," *Annals of the New York Academy of Sciences* 585 (1990), pp. 302–320.

6. John M. Ellis, "Vitamin B$_6$ in Treatment of the Carpal-Tunnel and Shoulder-Hand Syndromes," *Journal of Applied Nutrition* 24 (1972), pp. 75–86.

7. Kerry Pechter, "The Odd Disease That Wrecks Your Wrist," *Prevention*, April 1988, pp. 50–52.

8. John M. Ellis and James Presley, *Vitamin B$_6$: The Doctor's Report* (New York: Harper and Row, 1973), pp. 57–73.

9. Ware, pp. 7–9.

10. Ellis, pp. 75–86.

11. J.M. Ellis, K. Folkers, M. Levy, S. Schizukuishi, J. Lewandowski, S. Nishii, H. Shubert, and R. Ulrich, "Response of Vitamin B_6 Deficiency and the Carpal Tunnel Syndrome to Pyridoxine," *Proceedings of the National Academy of Sciences (Medical Sciences)* 79 (1982), pp. 7494–7498.

12. Ellis and Folkers, pp. 302–320.

13. Ellis, pp. 75–86.

14. J.J. Putnam, "A Series of Cases of Paresthesia, Mainly of the Hands, Periodical Recurrence, and Possibly of Vasomotor Origin," *Archives of Medicine* 4 (1980), pp. 147–162.

15. F. Schultze, "Über Akroparesthese" [About Acroparesthesia], *Nervenheily Deutsch* 3 (1993), pp. 300–318.

16. N. Taylor, "Special Review of Carpal-Tunnel Syndrome," *American Journal of Physical Medicine and Rehabilitation* 50 (1971), pp. 192–213.

17. B.W. Cannon and J.G. Love, "Tardy Median Palsy; Median Neuritis; Median Thenar Neuritis Amenable to Surgery," *Surgery* 20 (1946), pp. 210–216.

18. W.R. Brain, A.D. Wright, and M. Wilkinson, "Spontaneous Compression of Both Median Nerves in Carpal Tunnel," *Lancet* 1 (1947), pp. 277–282.

19. G.S. Phalen, "The Carpal-Tunnel Syndrome: Seventeen Years' Experience in Diagnosis and Treatment of Six Hundred Fifty-Four Hands," *Journal of Bone and Joint Surgery* 48A (1966), pp. 211–228.

20. S.M. Tobin, "Carpal-Tunnel Syndrome in Pregnancy," *American Journal of Physical Medicine and Rehabilitation* 97 (1967), pp. 493–498.

21. D.P. Rose, "Excretion of Xanthurenic Acid in the Urine of Women Taking Progestrogenoestrogen Preparations," *Nature* 210 (1966), pp. 196–197.

22. A.L. Luhby, P. Davis, M. Murphy, M. Gordon, M. Brin, and H. Spiegel, "Pyridoxine and Oral Contraceptives," *Lancet* 2 (1970), p. 1083.

23. Y. Kotake Jr. and Y. Inoto, "Studies on Xanthurenic Acid," part 2: "Preliminary Report on Xanthurenic Acid Diabetes," *Journal of Biochemistry* 40 (1953), p. 291.

24. Y. Kotake Jr. and Y. Inoto, "Studies on Xanthurenic Acid," part 10: "Progressive Depletion in the Reduced Glutathionine Content of the Blood Following Xanthurenic Acid Injection," *Journal of Biochemistry* 41 (1954), p. 627.

25. Y. Kotake Jr., "Experiments of Chronic Diabetes Symptoms Caused by Xanthurenic Acid, an Abnormal Metabolite of Tryptophan," *Clinical Chemistry* 3 (1957), p. 432.

26. Tobin, pp. 493–498.

27. Rose, pp. 196–197.

28. Luhby, Davis, Murphy, Gordon, Brin, and Spiegel, p. 1083.

29. "Studies on Xanthurenic Acid," part 2: "Preliminary Report on Xanthurenic Acid Diabetes," p. 291.

30. "Studies on Xanthurenic Acid," part 10: "Progressive Depletion in the Reduced Glutathionine Content of the Blood Following Xanthurenic Acid Injection," p. 627.

31. Kotake, p. 432.

Chapter 5
Gynecologic and Obstetric Disorders

1. Pauline Slovak, Pat Hamilton, and Jean Pamplin, editors, *Notions and Potions of East Texas* (Mt. Vernon, Texas: NeT Publishing, 1994), pp. 13–14.

2. H. Borsook, *Vitamins and Hormones* (New York: Academic Press, 1964), pp 855–874.

3. John Marion Ellis, "Pregnant Women Should Take Vitamin B$_6$," *Better Nutrition*, April 1984, pp. 12, 42–46.

4. "B Complex for a Comfortable Pregnancy," *Prevention*, December 1970, pp. 74–76.

5. Angela A. Powell and Marc A. Armstrong, "Peripheral Edema," *American Family Physician* 55 (April 1997), pp. 1721–1726.

6. J.M. Ellis, *The Doctor Who Looked at Hands* (New York: Vantage Press, 1966), pp. 147–153.

7. Eileen Mazer, "Natural Remedies for Fluid Retention," *Prevention*, December 1983, pp. 106–112.

8. John M. Ellis and James Presley, *Vitamin B$_6$: The Doctor's Report* (New York: Harper and Row, 1973), p. 209.

9. J.M. Ellis, "Treatment of Carpal Tunnel Syndrome With Vitamin B$_6$," *Southern Medical Journal* 80 (July 1987), pp. 882–884.

10. M. Wachstein and A. Gudaitis. "Disturbance of Vitamin B$_6$ Metabolism in Pregnancy," part 2: "The Influence of Various Amounts of Pyridoxine Hydrochloride Upon the Abnormal Tryptophan Load Test in Pregnant Women," *Journal of Laboratory and Clinical Medicine* 42 (1953), p. 98.

11. M. Wachstein and L.W. Graffeo, "Influence of Vitamin B$_6$ on the Incidence of Preeclampsia," *Obstetrics and Gynecology* 8 (1956), p. 177.

12. Bill Gottlieb, "Millions of Women Need More B$_6$," *Prevention*, April 1977, pp. 97–103.

13. J.A. Kleiger, C.H. Altshuler, G. Drakow, et al., "Abnormal Pyridoxine Metabolism in Toxemia of Pregnancy," *Annals of the New York Academy of Sciences* 166 (1969), pp. 288–296.

14. A. Kirksey and S.A. Udipi, "Vitamin B$_6$ in Human Pregnancy and Lactation," in R. Reynolds and J. Leklem, editors, *Vitamin B$_6$: Its Role in Health and Disease* (New York: Alan R. Liss, 1985), pp 57–77.

15. Gottlierb, pp. 97–103.

16. I. Quere, H. Bellet, M. Hoffet, C. Janbon, P. Mares, and J.C. Gris, "A Woman With 5 Consecutive Fetal Deaths: Case Report and Retrospective Analysis of Hyperhomocysteinemia Prevalence in 100 Consecutive Women With Recurrent Miscarriages," *Fertility and Sterility* 69 (January 1998), pp. 152–154.

17. "Pregnant Women Should Take Vitamin B$_6$," pp. 12, 42–46.

18. "Pregnant Women Should Take Vitamin B$_6$," pp. 12, 42–46.

19. K.P. Dolan, J.J. Diaz-Gil, and G. Litwack, "Interaction of Pyridoxal-5-Phosphate With the Liver Glucocorticoid Receptor–DNA Complex," *Archives of Biochemistry and Biophysics* 201 (1980), pp. 476–485.

20. G. Litwack, A. Miller-Diener, D.M. Disorbo, and T.J. Schmidt, "Vitamin B$_6$ and the Glucocorticoid Receptor," in R. Reynolds and J. Leklem, editors, *Vitamin B$_6$: Its Role in Health and Disease* (New York: Alan R. Liss, 1985), pp. 177–191.

21. D.M. Disorbo, D.S. Phelps, V.S. Ohl, and G. Litwack, "Pyridoxine Deficiency Influences the Behavior of the Glucocorticoid Receptor Complex," *Journal of Biological Chemistry* 255 (10 May 1980), pp. 3866–3870.

22. V.E. Allgood, F.E. Powell-Oliver, and J.A. Cidlowski, "The Influence of Vitamin B_6 on the Structure and Function of the Glucocorticoid Receptor," *Annals of the New York Academy of Sciences* 585 (1990), pp. 452–465.

23. D.B. Tulix, V.E. Allgood, and J.A. Cidlowski, "Modulation of Steroid Receptor–Mediated Gene Expression by Vitamin B_6," *The Federation of American Societies for Experimental Biology Journal* 8 (March 1994), pp. 343–349.

24. D.A. Bender, "Oestrogens and Vitamin B_6: Actions and Interactions," *World Review of Nutrition and Dietetics* 52 (1987), pp. 140–188.

25. Charles B. Hammond, "Management of Menopause," *American Family Physician* 55 (April 1997), pp 1667–1674.

26. John Marion Ellis, *Diabetes New Therapies: Clinically Proven Usage of Vitamin B_6* (Waco, Texas: Texian Press, 1995), p. 30.

27. "B Complex for a Comfortable Pregnancy," pp. 74–76.

Chapter 6
Diabetes

1. Carl Sherman, "The Prevalence of Diabetes Has Tripled Since 1960," *Family Practice News*, 15 January 1996, p. 6.

2. Diabetes Control and Complications Trial Research Group, "The Effect of Intensive Treatment of Diabetes on the Development and Progression of Long-Term Complications in Insulin-Dependent Diabetes Melli-

tus," *The New England Journal of Medicine* 329 (30 September 1993), pp. 977–986.

3. Bill Sardi, "Insulin and Laser vs. Diet and Nutritional Supplements," part 1: "The Disappointment of Modern Therapy," *Townsend Letter for Doctors and Patients*, April 1996, p. 72.

4. Diabetes Control and Complications Trial Research Group, pp. 977–986.

5. John M. Ellis and Harry Preston, *Free of Pain: The Cause of Soft Tissue Rheumatism*, revised edition update (Atlanta, Texas: Natural Food Associates, 1988), pp. 79–88.

6. K. Folkers, J. Ellis, T. Watanabe, S. Saji, and M. Kaji, "Biochemical Evidence for a Deficiency of Vitamin B_6 in the Carpal Tunnel Syndrome Based on a Cross-Over Clinical Study," *Proceedings of the National Academy of Sciences* (1978), pp. 3410–3412.

7. J.M. Ellis, K. Folkers, M. Levy, S. Schizukuishi, J. Lewandowski, S. Nishii, H. Shubert, and R. Ulrich, "Response of Vitamin B_6 Deficiency and the Carpal Tunnel Syndrome to Pyridoxine," *Proceedings of the National Academy of Sciences (Medical Sciences)* 79 (1982), pp. 7494–7498.

8. J.M. Ellis, "Treatment of Carpal Tunnel Syndrome With Vitamin B_6," *Southern Medical Journal* 80 (July 1987), pp. 882–884.

9. J.M. Ellis and K. Folkers, "Clinical Aspects of Treatment of Carpal Tunnel Syndrome With Vitamin B_6," *Annals of the New York Academy of Sciences* 585 (1990), pp. 302–320.

10. John M. Ellis, Karl Folkers, Michael Minadeo, Ronald Van Buskirk, Li-Jun Xia, and Hiroo Tamagawa, "A Defi-

ciency of Vitamin B_6 Is a Plausible Molecular Basis of the Retinopathy of Patients With Diabetes Mellitus, *Biochemical and Biophysical Research Communications* 179 (30 August 1991), pp. 615–619.

11. John Marion Ellis, *Diabetes New Therapies: Clinically Proven Usage of Vitamin B_6* (Waco, Texas: Texian Press, 1995), pp. 37–38.

12. John M. Ellis, Diabetic Blindness, *Diabetic Nephropathy: End Stages of Sustained Hyperglycemia and Long-Term Vitamin B_6 Deficiency* (Atlanta, Texas: Natural Food Associates, 1995), pp. 1–54.

13. J.M. Ellis, *The Doctor Who Looked at Hands* (New York: Vantage Press, 1966).

14. John M. Ellis, "Vitamin B_6 in Treatment of the Carpal-Tunnel and Shoulder-Hand Syndromes," *Journal of Applied Nutrition* 24 (1972), pp. 75–86.

15. John M. Ellis and James Presley, *Vitamin B_6: The Doctor's Report* (New York: Harper and Row, 1973), pp. 127–146.

16. G.S. Phalen, "Reflections on 21 Years Experience With the Carpal Tunnel Syndrome," *Journal of the American Medical Association* 212 (1970), pp. 1365–1367.

17. *Diabetes New Therapies: Clinically Proven Usage of Vitamin B_6*, pp. 37–38.

18. Sardi, p. 72.

19. Sherman, p. 6.

Chapter 7
Coronary Heart Disease

1. John M. Ellis and Kilmer S. McCully, "Prevention of Myocardial Infarction by Vitamin B_6," *Research Com-*

munications in Molecular Pathology and Pharmacology 89 (August 1995), pp. 208–220.

2. Jacob Selhub, Paul F. Jacques, Andrew G. Bostom, Ralph B. D'Agostino, Peter W.F. Wilson, Albert J. Belanger, Daniel H. O'Leary, Philip A. Wolf, Ernst J. Schaefer, and Irwin H. Rosenberg, "Association Between Plasma Homocysteine Concentrations and Extracranial Carotid-Artery Stenosis," *The New England Journal of Medicine* 332 (1995), pp. 286–291.

3. K.S. McCully, "Chemical Pathology of Homocysteine," part 1: "Atherogenesis," *Annals of Clinical and Laboratory Science* 23 (1993), pp. 477–493.

4. Kilmer S. McCully, "Homocysteine and Vascular Disease," *Nature Medicine* 2 (April, 1996), pp. 386–389.

5. Nina A.J. Carson, C.E. Dent, C.M.B. Field, and Gerald E. Gaull, "Homocystinuria: Clinical and Pathological Review of 10 Cases," *Journal of Pediatrics* 66 (1965), pp. 565–583.

6. Neal Konecky, M. Ren'e Malinow, Paul A. Tunick, Robin S. Freedberg, Barry P. Rosenzweig, Edward S. Katz, Davil L. Hess, Barbara Upson, Blanche Leung, John Perez, and Itzhak Kronzon, "Correlation Between Plasma Homocysteine and Aortic Atherosclerosis," *American Heart Journal* 133 (1997), pp. 534–540.

7. Stephen P. Coburn, "Modeling Vitamin B₆ Metabolism," *Advances in Food and Nutrition Research* 40 (1996), pp. 107–132.

8. Gary Evans, *Chromium Picolinate: Everything You Need to Know* (Garden City Park, New York: Avery Publishing Group, 1996).

9. Denise Mann, "'Normal' Homocysteine, Low B$_6$ May Raise CHD Risk," *Medical Tribune*, 11 January 1996, p. 5.

10. K. Robinson, E. Mayer, M. Miller, R. Green, F. Lente, A. Gupta, K. Kottke-Marchant, S. Savon, J. Selub, S. Nissen, M. Kutner, E. Topol, and D. Jacobson, "Hyperhomocysteinemia and Low Pyridoxal Phosphate Common and Independent Reversible Risk Factors for Coronary Artery Disease," *Circulation* 92 (15 November 1995), pp. 2825–2830.

11. Kilmer S. McCully, *The Homocysteine Revolution* (New Canaan, Connecticut: Keats Publishing, 1997).

12. H.H. Moghadasian, B.M. McManus, and J.J. Frohlich, "Homocysteine and Coronary Artery Disease," *Archives of Internal Medicine* 157 (10 November 1997), pp. 2299–2308.

13. R.S. Ballal, D.W. Jacobsen, and K. Robinson, "Homocysteine: Update on a New Risk Factor," *Cleveland Clinic Journal of Medicine* 64 (November/December 1997), pp. 543–549.

Chapter 8
Arthritis and Rheumatism

1. John M. Ellis and Harry Preston, *Free of Pain: The Cause of Soft Tissue Rheumatism*, revised edition update (Atlanta, Texas: Natural Food Associates, 1988).

2. John M. Ellis, "Defend Yourself Against Vitamin B$_6$ Deficiency," *Better Nutrition*, August 1985, pp. 14–17, 27.

3. Stephen P. Coburn, "Modeling Vitamin B$_6$ Metabolism," *Advances in Food and Nutrition Research* 40 (1996), pp. 107–132.

4. J.C. Murray, D.R. Fraser, and C.I. Levene, "The Effect of Pyridoxine Deficiency on Lysyl Oxidase Activity in the Chick," *Experimental and Molecular Pathology* 28 (1978), pp. 301–308.

5. P.G. Masse, F. Gerber, V.E. Colombo, and H. Weiser, "Ultrastructural Defects in the Cartilage Collagen Caused by Vitamin B$_6$ Deficiency," *Annals of the New York Academy of Sciences* 585 (1990), pp. 522–525.

6. C.H. Hill and Chun Su Kim, "The Derangement of Elastin Synthesis in Pyridoxine Deficiency," *Biochemical and Biophysical Research Communications* 27 (1997), pp. 94–99.

7. D.M. Yamaguchi, P.R. Lipscomb, and E.H. Soule, "Carpal Tunnel Syndrome," *Minnesota Medicine* 48 (1965), pp. 22–23.

8. G.S. Phalen, "Reflections on 21 Years Experience With the Carpal Tunnel Syndrome," *Journal of the American Medical Association* 212 (1970), pp. 1365–1367.

9. J.M. Ellis, "Treatment of Carpal Tunnel Syndrome With Vitamin B$_6$," *Southern Medical Journal* 80 (July 1987), pp. 882–884.

10. John Marion Ellis, "More Reasons for Taking Vitamin B$_6$," *Better Nutrition*, March 1984, pp. 10–11, 44, 46.

11. M.E. Brunet, Lyle A. Norwood, and Ted F. Sykes, "What to Do for the Painful Shoulder," *Patient Care*, 15 January 1997, pp. 56–83.

12. K. Rogers and S. Evangelista, "3-Hydroxykynurenine, 3-Hydroxyanthranilic Acid, and 0-Aminophenol Inhibit Leucine-Stimulated Insulin Release From Rat Pancreatic Islets," *Proceedings of the Society of Experimental Biology and Medicine* 178 (1985), pp. 275–278.

13. K.S. McCully, "Homocysteine Theory of Arteriosclerosis: Development and Current Status," in A.M. Gotto Jr. and R. Paoletti, editors, *Atherosclerosis Reviews*, volume 11 (New York: Raven Press, 1983), pp. 157–246.

Chapter 9
Brain Function

1. Abraham White, Philip Handler, Emil L. Smith, and DeWitt Stetten Jr., *Principles of Biochemistry*, second edition (New York: McGraw-Hill, 1959), p. 567.

2. Mary Coleman, "Studies of the Administration of Pyridoxine to Children With Down's Syndrome," in *Clinical and Physiological Applications of Vitamin B_6* (New York: Alan R. Liss, 1987), pp. 317–328.

3. B. Rimland, E. Callaway, and P. Dreyfus, "The Effects of High Doses of Vitamin B_6 on Autistic Children: A Double-Blind Study," *American Journal of Psychiatry* 135 (1978), pp. 472–475.

4. C. Barthelemy, J. Martineau, N. Bruneau, J.P. Muh, G. LeLord, and E. Callaway, "Clinical and Biological Effects of Pyridoxine Plus Magnesium in Autistic Subjects," in *Clinical and Physiological Applications of Vitamin B_6* (New York: Alan R. Liss, 1987), pp. 329–356.

5. A.F. Heeley and G.E. Roberts, "Tryptophan Metabolism in Psychotic Children: A Preliminary Report," *Developmental Medicine and Child Neurology* 7 (1965), pp. 46–49.

6. G. Ellman, "Pyridoxine Effectiveness on Autistic Patients at Sonoma State Hospital," abstract, in *Proceedings of the Research Conference on Autism*, 1981.

7. Bernard Rimland, "Vitamin B_6 (and Magnesium) in the Treatment of Autism," editorial, Autism Research Review International 1 (1994).

8. J.M. Ellis, "Treatment of Carpal Tunnel Syndrome With Vitamin B$_6$," *Southern Medical Journal* 80 (July 1987), pp. 882–884.

9. D.B. Coursin, *Journal of the American Medical Assocication* 154 (1954), pp. 406–408.

10. A. Kirksey, D.M. Morre, and A.Z. Wasynczuk, "Neuronal Development in Vitamin B$_6$ Deficiency," *Annals of the New York Academy of Sciences* 585 (1990), pp. 202–218.

Chapter 10
Dietary Factors Involving Vitamin B$_6$

1. L.M. Morrison, "Diet in Coronary Atherosclerosis," *Journal of the American Medical Association* 173 (25 June 1960), pp. 884–888.

2. John M. Ellis, "Addendum A: Development of Food Products," in *Proceedings, Western Hemisphere Nutrition Congress* (Chicago: American Medical Association, 1966), pp. 247–248.

3. J.M. Ellis, *The Doctor Who Looked at Hands* (New York: Vantage Press, 1966), pp. 147–153, 147–150.

Chapter 11
Your Complete Nutritional Program

1. H. Schaumburg, J. Kaplan, A. Windebank, et al., "Sensory Neurophathy from Pyridoxine Abuse: A New Megavitamin Syndrome," *New England Journal of Medicine* 309 (1983), pp. 445–448.

2. A.L. Bernstein, "Vitamin B$_6$ in Clinical Neurology," Annals of the New York Academy of Sciences 585 (1990), pp. 250–260.

Conclusion

1. Milton Kochler, "B$_6$—The Vitamin That Vanishes With Youth," *Prevention*, March 1973, pp. 79–84.

2. Bill Gottlierb, "Millions of Women Need More B$_6$," *Prevention*, April 1977, pp. 97–103.

3. Sherry Boschert, "Child Nutrition Guidelines Needed," *Family Practice News* 27 (15 January 1997), p. 40.

4. Joanne N. Hough, letter to author, 7 February 1994.

5. Bill Francis, letter to Food and Drug Administration, Department of Health and Social Services, 29 September 1995.

6. David Ponsonby, letter to Food and Drug Administration, Department of Health and Social Services, 1995.

7. John M. Ellis, petition to Food and Drug Administration, Department of Health and Social Services, 4 December 1995.

BIBLIOGRAPHY

Books

Borsook, H. *Vitamins and Hormones.* New York: Academic Press, 1964.

Ellis, J.M. *The Doctor Who Looked at Hands.* New York: Vantage Press, 1966.

Ellis, John M. *Diabetic Blindness, Diabetic Nephropathy: End Stages of Sustained Hyperglycemia and Long-Term Vitamin B_6 Deficiency.* Atlanta, Texas: Natural Food Associates, 1995.

_____. *Free of Pain: The Cause of Soft Tissue Rheumatism,* revised edition update. Dallas: Southwest Publishing Co., 1983.

Ellis, John M., and James Presley. *Vitamin B_6: The Doctor's Report.* New York: Harper and Row, 1973.

Ellis, John M., and Harry Preston. *Free of Pain: The Cause of Soft Tissue Rheumatism,* revised edition update. Atlanta, Texas: Natural Food Associates, 1988.

Ellis, John Marion. *Diabetes New Therapies: Clinically Proven Usage of Vitamin B_6.* Waco, Texas: Texian Press, 1995.

Evans, Gary. *Chromium Picolinate: Everything You Need to Know*. Garden City Park, New York: Avery Publishing Group, 1996.

McCully, Kilmer S. *The Homocysteine Revolution*. New Canaan, Connecticut: Keats Publishing, 1997.

Shabert, Judy, and Nancy Ehrlich. *The Ultimate Nutrient Glutamine: The Essential Nonessential Amino Acid*. Garden City Park, New York: Avery Publishing Group, 1994.

Slovak, Pauline; Pat Hamilton; and Jean Pamplin, editors. *Notions and Potions of East Texas*. Mt. Vernon, Texas: NeT Publishing, 1994.

White, Abraham; Philip Handler; Emil L. Smith; and DeWitt Stetten Jr. *Principles of Biochemistry*, second edition. New York: McGraw-Hill, 1959.

Articles

Allgood, V.E.; F.E. Powell-Oliver; and J.A. Cidlowski. "The Influence of Vitamin B₆ on the Structure and Function of the Glucocorticoid Receptor." *Annals of the New York Academy of Sciences* 585 (1990), pp. 452–465.

"B Complex for a Comfortable Pregnancy." *Prevention*, December 1970, pp. 74–76.

Ballal, R.S.; D.W. Jacobsen; and K. Robinson. "Homocysteine: Update on a New Risk Factor." *Cleveland Clinic Journal of Medicine* 64 (November/December 1997), pp. 543–549.

Bender, D.A. "Oestrogens and Vitamin B₆: Actions and Interactions." *World Review of Nutrition and Dietetics* 52 (1987), pp. 140–188.

Bernstein, A.L. "Vitamin B₆ in Clinical Neurology." *Annals of the New York Academy of Sciences* 585 (1990), pp. 250–260.

Boschert, Sherry. "Child Nutrition Guidelines Needed." *Family Practice News* 27 (15 January 1997), p. 40.

Boston, A.G.; R.Y. Gohh; A.J. Beaulieu; M.R. Nadeau; A.L. Hume; P.F. Jacques; J. Seleub; and I.H. Rosenberg. "Treatment of Hyperhomocysteinemia in Renal Transplant Patients." *Annals of Internal Medicine* 127 (December 1997), pp. 1089–1092.

Brain, W.R.; A.D. Wright; and M. Wilkinson. "Spontaneous Compression of Both Median Nerves in Carpal Tunnel." *Lancet* 1 (1947), pp. 277–282.

Brown, R.R. "Normal and Pathological Conditions Which May Alter the Human Requirement for Vitamin B_6." *Journal of Agriculture and Food Chemistry*, n.d.

Brunet, M.E.; Lyle A. Norwood; and Ted F. Sykes. "What to Do for the Painful Shoulder." *Patient Care*, 15 January 1997, pp. 56–83.

Cannon, B.W., and J.G. Love. "Tardy Median Palsy; Median Neuritis; Median Thenar Neuritis Amenable to Surgery." *Surgery* 20 (1946), pp. 210–216.

Carson, Nina A.J.; C.E. Dent; C.M.B. Field; and Gerald E. Gaull. "Homocystinuria: Clinical and Pathological Review of 10 Cases." *Journal of Pediatrics* 66 (1965), pp. 565–583.

Coburn. Stephen P. "Modeling Vitamin B_6 Metabolism." *Advances in Food and Nutrition Research* 40 (1996), pp. 107–132.

Coursin, D.B. *Journal of the American Medical Association* 154 (1954), pp. 406–408.

Diabetes Control and Complications Trial Research Group. "The Effect of Intensive Treatment of Diabetes on the Development and Progression of Long-Term Complications in Insulin-Dependent Diabetes Mellitus." *The New England Journal of Medicine* 329 (30 September 1993), pp. 977–986.

Disorbo, D.M.; D.S. Phelps; V.S. Ohl; and G. Litwack. "Pyridoxine Deficiency Influences the Behavior of the Glucocorticoid Receptor Complex." *Journal of Biological Chemistry* 255 (10 May 1980), pp. 3866–3870.

Dolan, K.P.; J.J. Diaz-Gil; and G. Litwack. "Interaction of Pyridoxal-5-Phosphate With the Liver Glucocorticoid Receptor–DNA Complex." *Archives of Biochemistry and Biophysics* 201 (1980), pp. 476–485.

Ellis, J.M. "Treatment of Carpal Tunnel Syndrome With Vitamin B$_6$." *Southern Medical Journal* 80 (July 1987), pp. 882–884.

Ellis, J.M., and K. Folkers. "Clinical Aspects of Treatment of Carpal Tunnel Syndrome With Vitamin B$_6$." *Annals of the New York Academy of Sciences* 585 (1990), pp. 302–320.

Ellis, J.M.; K. Folkers; M. Levy; S. Schizukuishi; J. Lewandowski; S. Nishii; H. Shubert; and R. Ulrich. "Response of Vitamin B$_6$ Deficiency and the Carpal Tunnel Syndrome to Pyridoxine." *Proceedings of the National Academy of Sciences (Medical Sciences)* 79 (1982), pp. 7494–7498.

Ellis, John M. "Defend Yourself Against Vitamin B$_6$ Deficiency." *Better Nutrition*, August 1985, pp. 14–17, 27.

_____."Vitamin B$_6$ in Treatment of the Carpal-Tunnel and Shoulder-Hand Syndromes." *Journal of Applied Nutrition* 24 (1972), pp. 75–86.

Ellis, John M.; Karl Folkers; Michael Minadeo; Ronald Van Buskirk; Li-Jun Xia; and Hiroo Tamagawa. "A Deficiency of Vitamin B$_6$ Is a Plausible Molecular Basis of the Retinopathy of Patients With Diabetes Mellitus." *Biochemical and Biophysical Research Communications* 179 (30 August 1991), pp. 615–619.

Ellis, John M., and Kilmer S. McCully. "Prevention of Myocardial Infarction by Vitamin B_6." *Research Communications in Molecular Pathology and Pharmacology* 89 (August 1995), pp. 208–220.

Ellis, John Marion. "More Reasons for Taking Vitamin B_6." *Better Nutrition*, March 1984, pp. 10–11, 44, 46.

_____."Pregnant Women Should Take Vitamin B_6." *Better Nutrition*, April 1984, pp. 12, 42–46.

Evans, G.W. "Effect of Chromium Picolinate on Insulin Controlled Parameters in Humans." *International Journal of Biosocial and Medical Research* 11 (1989), pp. 163–180.

_____."An Inexpensive, Convenient Adjunct for the Treatment of Diabetes." *Western Journal of Medicine* 155 (1991), p. 549.

Folkers, K.; J. Ellis; T. Watanabe; S. Saji; and M. Kaji. "Biochemical Evidence for a Deficiency of Vitamin B_6 in the Carpal Tunnel Syndrome Based on a Cross-Over Clinical Study." *Proceedings of the National Academy of Sciences* (1978), pp. 3410–3412.

Glassford, Howard. "Report." *Today's Health* (December 1954), pp. 26–27, 44.

Gottlierb, Bill. "Millions of Women Need More B_6." *Prevention*, April 1977, pp. 97–103.

Gupta, A.; A. Moustapha; D.W. Jacobsen; M. Goormastic; E.M. Tuzcu; R. Hobbs; J. Young; K. James; P. McCarthy; F. Vanlente; R. Green; and K. Robinson. "High Homocysteine, Low Folate, and Low Vitamin B_6 Concentrations: Prevelant Risk Factors for Vascular Disease in Heart Transplant Recipients." *Transplantation* 65 (27 February 1998), pp. 544–550.

György, Paul. "Developments Leading to the Metabolic Role of Vitamin B₆." *American Journal of Clinical Nutrition* 24 (October 1971), pp. 1250–1256.

_____."The History of Vitamin B₆: Introductory Remarks." *Vitamins and Hormones* 22 (1964), pp. 361–365.

Hammond, Charles B. "Management of Menopause." *American Family Physician* 55 (April 1997), pp 1667–1674.

Harris, John W., and Daniel L. Horrigan. "Pyridoxine-Responsive Anemia: Prototype and Variations on the Theme." *Vitamins and Hormones* 22 (1964), pp. 721–753.

Heeley, A.F., and G.E. Roberts. "Tryptophan Metabolism in Psychotic Children: A Preliminary Report." *Developmental Medicine and Child Neurology* 7 (1965), pp. 46–49.

Hill, C.H., and Chun Su Kim. "The Derangement of Elastin Synthesis in Pyridoxine Deficiency." *Biochemical and Biophysical Research Communications* 27 (1997), pp. 94–99.

Khatami, M. "Role of Pyridoxal Phosphate/Pyridoxine in Diabetes." *Annals of the New York Academy of Sciences* 585 (1990), pp 502–504.

Kirksey, A.; D.M. Morre; and A.Z. Wasynczuk. "Neuronal Development in Vitamin B₆ Deficiency." *Annals of the New York Academy of Sciences* 585 (1990), pp. 202–218.

Kleiger, J.A.; C.H. Altshuler; G. Drakow; et al. "Abnormal Pyridoxine Metabolism in Toxemia of Pregnancy." *Annals of the New York Academy of Sciences* 166 (1969), pp. 288–296.

Kochler, Milton. "B₆—The Vitamin That Vanishes With Youth." *Prevention*, March 1973, pp. 79–84.

Konecky, Neal; M. Ren'e Malinow; Paul A. Tunick; Robin S. Freedberg; Barry P. Rosenzweig; Edward S. Katz; Davil L. Hess; Barbara Upson; Blanche Leung; John Perez; and Itzhak Kronzon. "Correlation Between Plasma Homocysteine and Aortic Atherosclerosis." *American Heart Journal* 133 (1997), pp. 534–540.

Kotake, Y., Jr. "Experiments of Chronic Diabetes Symptoms Caused by Xanthurenic Acid, an Abnormal Metabolite of Tryptophan." *Clinical Chemistry* 3 (1957), p. 432.

Kotake, Y., Jr., and Y. Inoto. "Studies on Xanthurenic Acid," part 2: "Preliminary Report on Xanthurenic Acid Diabetes." *Journal of Biochemistry* 40 (1953), p. 291.

Kotake, Y., Jr., and Y. Inoto. "Studies on Xanthurenic Acid," part 10: "Progressive Depletion in the Reduced Glutathionine Content of the Blood Following Xanthurenic Acid Injection." *Journal of Biochemistry* 41 (1954), p. 627.

Lepkovsky, Samuel; Elisabeth Roboz; and A.J. Haagen-Smit. "Xanthurenic Acid and Its Role in the Tryptophan Metabolism of Pyridoxine-Deficient Rats." *Journal of Biological Chemistry* 149 (1943), pp. 195–201.

Lu, J.Y.; D.L. Cook; J.B. Jarvis; Z.A. Kirmani; C.C. Liu; D.N. Makadia; T.A. Makadam; O.B. Omasayie; D.P. Patel; V.J. Reddy; B.W. Walker; C.S. Williams; and R.A. Chung. "Intakes of Vitamins and Minerals by Pregnant Women With Selected Clinical Symptoms." *Journal of the American Diabetic Association* 78 (May 1981), pp. 477–481.

Luhby, A.L.; P. Davis; M. Murphy; M. Gordon; M. Brin; and H. Spiegel. "Pyridoxine and Oral Contraceptives." *Lancet* 2 (1970), p. 1083.

Mann, Denise. "'Normal' Homocysteine, Low B_6 May Raise CHD Risk." *Medical Tribune*, 11 January 1996, p. 5.

Masse, P.G.; F. Gerber; V.E. Colombo; and H. Weiser. "Ultrastructural Defects in the Cartilage Collagen Caused by Vitamin B_6 Deficiency." *Annals of the New York Academy of Sciences* 585 (1990), pp. 522–525.

Mather, H.M.; G.E. Levin; and J.A. Nisbet. "Hypomagnesemia and Symptomatic Ischemic Heart Disease in Diabetes." *Magnesium Bulletin* 3 (1981), pp. 169–172.

Mazer, Eileen. "Natural Remedies for Fluid Retention." *Prevention*, December 1983, pp. 106–112.

McCully, K.S. "Chemical Pathology of Homocysteine," part 1: "Atherogenesis." *Annals of Clinical and Laboratory Science* 23 (1993), pp. 477–493.

_____."Vascular Pathology of Homocysteinemia: Implications for the Pathogenesis of Arteriosclerosis." *American Journal of Pathology* 66 (1969), pp. 111–128.

McCully, Kilmer S. "Homocysteine, Folate, Vitamin B_6, and Cardiovascular Disease." *Journal of the American Medical Association* 279 (4 February 1998), pp. 392–393.

_____."Homocysteine and Vascular Disease." *Nature Medicine* 2 (April, 1996), pp. 386–389.

McNair, P.; C. Christiansen; C. Madsbad; et al. "Hypomagnesemia: A Risk Factor in Diabetic Retinopathy." *Diabetes* 27 (1978), pp. 1075–1077.

Meyer, Ann. "Carpal Tunnel Syndrome: Surprise—You May Be At Risk." *Better Homes and Gardens*, June 1991, pp. 38, 40.

Moghadasian, H.H.; B.M. McManus; and J.J. Frohlich. "Homocysteine and Coronary Artery Disease." *Archives of Internal Medicine* 157 (10 November 1997), pp. 2299–2308.

Monsen, E.R. "The 10th Edition of the Recommended Dietary Allowances (RDAs) 1989." *Journal of the American Dietetic Association* 89 (December 1989), pp. 1748–1752.

Morrison, L.M. "Diet in Coronary Atherosclerosis." *Journal of the American Medical Association* 173 (25 June 1960), pp. 884–888.

Mudd, S.H.; F. Skovby; H.L. Levy; K.D. Pettigrew; B. Wilcken; R.E. Pyeritz; G. Andria; G.H.J. Boers; I.L. Bromberg; R. Cerone; B. Fowler; H. Grobe; H. Schmidt; and L. Schweitzer. "The Natural History of Homocystinuria Due to Cystathionine Beta Synthase Deficiency." *American Journal of Human Genetics* 37 (1985), pp. 1–31.

Murray, J.C.; D.R. Fraser; and C.I. Levene. "The Effect of Pyridoxine Deficiency on Lysyl Oxidase Activity in the Chick." *Experimental and Molecular Pathology* 28 (1978), pp. 301–308.

Orey, Cal. "Preventing Carpal Tunnel Syndrome." *Fitness Plus— Better Health for Every Body*, March 1991, pp. 66, 124.

Paris, Paul. "Treating Diabetes With B_6." *Longview News-Journal*, 19 October 1995, pp. 1D–2D.

Pechter, Kerry. "The Odd Disease That Wrecks Your Wrist." *Prevention*, April 1988, pp. 50–52.

Phalen, G.S. "The Carpal-Tunnel Syndrome: Seventeen Years' Experience in Diagnosis and Treatment of Six Hundred Fifty-Four Hands." *Journal of Bone and Joint Surgery* 48A (1966), pp. 211–228.

_____."Reflections on 21 Years Experience With the Carpal Tunnel Syndrome." *Journal of the American Medical Association* 212 (1970), pp. 1365–1367.

Powell, Angela A., and Marc A. Armstrong. "Peripheral Edema." *American Family Physician* 55 (April 1997), pp. 1721–1726.

Putnam, J.J. "A Series of Cases of Paresthesia, Mainly of the Hands, Periodical Recurrence, and Possibly of Vaso-motor Origin." *Archives of Medicine* 4 (1980), pp. 147–162.

Quere, I.; H. Bellet; M. Hoffet; C. Janbon; P. Mares; and J.C. Gris. "A Woman With 5 Consecutive Fetal Deaths: Case Report and Retrospective Analysis of Hyperhomocysteinemia Prevalence in 100 Consecutive Women With Recurrent Miscarriages." *Fertility and Sterility* 69 (January 1998), pp. 152–154.

Ribaya-Mercado, J.D., et al. "Vitamin B$_6$ Requirement of Elderly Men and Women." *Journal of Nutrition* 121 (1991), pp. 1062–1074.

Rimland, B. "Controversies in the Treatment of Autistic Children: Vitamin and Drug Therapy." *Journal of Child Neurology* 3 (1988), supplement, pp. 568–572.

Rimland, B.; E. Callaway; and P. Dreyfus. "The Effects of High Doses of Vitamin B$_6$ on Autistic Children: A Double-Blind Study." *American Journal of Psychiatry* 135 (1978), pp. 472–475.

Rimland, Bernard. "Vitamin B$_6$ (and Magnesium) in the Treatment of Autism." Editorial. *Autism Research Review International* 1 (1994).

Rimm, E.B.; W.W. Willet; B. Frank; L. Sampson; A. Graham; M.B. Colditz; J.E. Manson; S. Henneken; and M.J. Stamfer. "Folate and Vitamin B$_6$ from Diet and Supplements in Relation to Risk of Coronary Heart Disease Among Women." *Journal of the American Medical Association* 279 (4 February 1998), pp. 358–364.

Rinehart, J.F., and L.D. Greenberg. "Pathogenesis of Experimental Arteriosclerosis in Pyridoxine Deficiency: With Notes on Similarities to Human Arteriosclerosis." *Archives of Pathology* 51 (1951), pp. 12–18.

Robinson, K.; E. Mayer; M. Miller; R. Green; F. Lente; A. Gupta; K. Kottke-Marchant; S. Savon; J. Selub; S. Nissen; M. Kutner; E. Topol; and D. Jacobson. "Hyperhomocysteinemia and Low Pyridoxal Phosphate Common and Independent Reversible Risk Factors for Coronary Artery Disease." *Circulation* 92 (15 November 1995), pp. 2825–2830.

Rogers, K., and S. Evangelista. "3-Hydroxykynurenine, 3-Hydroxyanthranilic Acid, and 0-Aminophenol Inhibit Leucine-Stimulated Insulin Release From Rat Pancreatic Islets." *Proceedings of the Society of Experimental Biology and Medicine* 178 (1985), pp. 275–278.

Rogers, K., and C. Mohan. "Mini-Review Vitamin B_6 Metabolism and Diabetes." *Biochemical Medicine and Metabolic Biology* 52 (1994), pp. 10–17.

Rogers, K.S.; E.S. Higgins; and E.S. Kline. "Experimental Diabetes Causes Mitochondrial Loss and Cytoplasmic Enrichment of Pyridoxal Phosphate and Aspartate Aminotransferase Activity." *Biochemical Medicine and Metabolic Biology* 36 (1986), pp. 91–97.

Rose, D.P. "Excretion of Xanthurenic Acid in the Urine of Women Taking Progestrogenoestrogen Preparations." *Nature* 210 (1966), pp. 196–197.

Sardi, Bill. "Insulin and Laser vs. Diet and Nutritional Supplements," part 1: "The Disappointment of Modern Therapy." *Townsend Letter for Doctors and Patients,* April 1996, p. 72.

Schaumburg, H.; J. Kaplan; A. Windebank; et al. "Sensory Neurophathy from Pyridoxine Abuse: A New Megavitamin Syndrome." *New England Journal of Medicine* 309 (1983), pp. 445–448.

Schultze, F. "Über Akroparesthese" [About Acroparesthesia]. *Nervenheily Deutsch* 3 (1993), pp. 300–318.

Science News Letter, 1 June 1940, p. 340.

Selhub, Jacob; Paul F. Jacques; Andrew G. Bostom; Ralph B. D'Agostino; Peter W.F. Wilson; Albert J. Belanger; Daniel H. O'Leary; Philip A. Wolf; Ernst J. Schaefer; and Irwin H. Rosenberg. "Association Between Plasma Homocysteine Concentrations and Extracranial Carotid-Artery Stenosis." *The New England Journal of Medicine* 332 (1995), pp. 286–291.

"Serendipitous Sulphonylureas." *Journal of the American Medical Association* 219 (6 March 1972), p. 1335.

Shepard, D.C.; J.B. Hitz; and J.A. Dain. "Pyridoxal-5-Phosphate Inhibits Nonenzymatic Glycosylation of Proteins." *Biochemical Archives* 1 (1985), pp. 143–151.

Sherman, Carl. "The Prevalence of Diabetes Has Tripled Since 1960." *Family Practice News*, 15 January 1996, p. 6.

Sjogren, A.; C.-H. Floren; and A. Nilsson. "Magnesium Deficiency in IDDM Related to Level of Glycosylated Hemoglobin." *Diabetes* 35 (1986), pp. 459–463.

Snell, Esmond E. "Summary of Session I and Some Notes on the Metabolism of Vitamin B₆." *Vitamins and Hormones* 22 (1964), pp. 485–494.

Solomon, L.R., and K. Cohen. "Erythrocyte 02 Transport and Metabolism and Effects of Vitamin B₆ Therapy in Type II Diabetes Mellitus." *Diabetes* 38 (July 1989), pp. 881–886.

Spies, Tom D.; William B. Bean; and William F. Ashe. "A Note on the Use of Vitamin B₆ in Human Nutrition." *Journal of the American Medical Association* (10 June 1939), pp. 2414–2415.

Stamfer, M.; M. Malinow; W. Willett; L. Newcomer; B. Upson; D. Ullmann; P. Tishler; and C. Hennekens. "A Prospective Study of Plasma Homocysteine and Risk of Myocardial Infarction in U.S. Physicians." *Journal of the American Medical Association* 270 (1992), pp. 2693–2698.

Suzman, M.M. "Effect of Pyridoxine and Low Animal Protein Diet in Coronary Heart Disease." *Circulation* 48 (1973), supplement IV, p. 254.

Taylor, N. "Special Review of Carpal-Tunnel Syndrome." *American Journal of Physical Medicine and Rehabilitation* 50 (1971), pp. 192–213.

Tobin, S.M. "Carpal-Tunnel Syndrome in Pregnancy." *American Journal of Physical Medicine and Rehabilitation* 97 (1967), pp. 493–498.

Tulix, D.B.; V.E. Allgood; and J.A. Cidlowski. "Modulation of Steroid Receptor–Mediated Gene Expression by Vitamin B_6." *The Federation of American Societies for Experimental Biology Journal* 8 (March 1994), pp. 343–349.

"24-Hour Recoveries Result From Synthesized Vitamin." *Science News Letter,* 24 June 1939, p. 395.

Vilter, Richard W. "The Vitamin B_6–Hydrazide Relationship." *Vitamins and Hormones* 22 (1964), pp. 797–805.

Wachstein, M., and L.W. Graffeo. "Influence of Vitamin B_6 on the Incidence of Preeclampsia." *Obstetrics and Gynecology* 8 (1956), p. 177.

Wachstein, M., and A. Gudaitis. "Disturbance of Vitamin B_6 Metabolism in Pregnancy," part 2: "The Influence of Various Amounts of Pyridoxine Hydrochloride Upon the Abnormal Tryptophan Load Test in Pregnant Women." *Journal of Laboratory and Clinical Medicine* 42 (1953), p. 98.

Wachstein, Max. "Evidence for a Relative Vitamin B_6 Deficiency in Pregnancy and Some Disease States." *Vitamins and Hormones* 22 (1964), pp. 705–719.

Ware, Ralph. "Carpal Tunnel Syndrome." *Natural Food and Farming,* January-February 1993, pp. 7–9.

Yamaguchi, D.M.; P.R. Lipscomb; and E.H. Soule. "Carpal Tunnel Syndrome." *Minnesota Medicine* 48 (1965), pp. 22–23.

Zoler, Mitchel L. "Folic Acid Cuts Homocysteine Levels in CV Disease." *Family Practice News*, 15 January 1997, pp. 20a–20b.

Miscellaneous Items

Barthelemy, C.; J. Martineau; N. Bruneau; J.P. Muh; G. LeLord; and E. Callaway. "Clinical and Biological Effects of Pyridoxine Plus Magnesium in Autistic Subjects." In *Clinical and Physiological Applications of Vitamin B₆* (New York: Alan R. Liss, 1987), pp. 329–356.

Braunstein, A.E. "Pyridoxal Phosphate." In P.D. Boyer; H.A. Lardy; and K. Myrback, editors, *The Enzymes*, volume 2 (New York: Academic Press, 1960), pp. 113–184.

Coleman, Mary. "Studies of the Administration of Pyridoxine to Children With Down's Syndrome." In *Clinical and Physiological Applications of Vitamin B₆* (New York: Alan R. Liss, 1987), pp. 317–328.

Ellis, John M. "Addendum A: Development of Food Products." In *Proceedings, Western Hemisphere Nutrition Congress* (Chicago: American Medical Association, 1966), pp. 247–248.

————. Petition to Food and Drug Administration, Department of Health and Social Services, 4 December 1995.

Ellman, G. "Pyridoxine Effectiveness on Autistic Patients at Sonoma State Hospital," abstract. In *Proceedings of the Research Conference on Autism*, 1981.

Francis, Bill. Letter to Food and Drug Administration, Department of Health and Social Services, 29 September 1995.

Hough, Joanne N. Letter to author, 7 February 1994.

Kirksey, A., and S.A. Udipi. "Vitamin B_6 in Human Pregnancy and Lactation." In R. Reynolds and J. Leklem, editors, *Vitamin B_6: Its Role in Health and Disease* (New York: Alan R. Liss, 1985), pp. 57–77.

Litwack, G.; A. Miller-Diener; D.M. Disorbo; and T.J. Schmidt. "Vitamin B_6 and the Glucocorticoid Receptor." In R. Reynolds and J. Leklem, editors, *Vitamin B_6: Its Role in Health and Disease* (New York: Alan R. Liss, 1985), pp. 177–191.

McCully, K.S. "Homocysteine Theory of Arteriosclerosis: Development and Current Status." In A.M. Gotto Jr. and R. Paoletti, editors, *Atherosclerosis Reviews*, volume 11 (New York: Raven Press, 1983), pp. 157–246.

Ponsonby, David. Letter to Food and Drug Administration, Department of Health and Social Services, 1995.

"Vitamin B_6 in Human Nutrition." In *Report of the Tenth M & R Pediatric Research Conference* (Columbus, Ohio: M & R Laboratories, 1954) p. 59.

ABOUT THE AUTHORS

John Marion Ellis was born June 1, 1917, in Oklahoma City, Oklahoma, and reared in Mt. Pleasant, Texas. He received his B.S. degree from Texas A. and M. University and M.D. degree from the University of Texas School of Medicine. For five years, he trained in medicine, pathology, and general surgery as an intern and resident physician at St. Louis City Hospital, Missouri Pacific Railroad Hospital, and Barnard  Skin and Cancer Hospital, St. Louis. During World War II, Dr. Ellis served as a medical officer in the U.S. Army Medical Corps. In Europe, he was appointed a special investigator with the International War Crimes Commission. In 1961, Dr. Ellis began his research with vitamin B_6. Today, he is the medical director of clinical research at Titus County Regional Medical Center, Mt. Pleasant, Texas.

Jean Pamplin is an author and publisher specializing in research and compilation projects. She lectures and helps to promote literary awareness through such means as Einstein's lesser known theory, "Imagination is greater than knowledge."

INDEX